On the Nature of Things

T. Edward Abbott

TINY BOAR BOOKS   PORT TOWNSEND, WA   2020

Tiny Boar Books
Water Street
Port Townsend, WA 98368
www.tinyboarbooks.com

The Library of Congress has catalogued this edition as follows:
    Abbott, T. Edward
        On the nature of things / T. Edward Abbott -1st Tiny Boar
Books ed.
        1. Magical Realism—Fiction. 2. Fairy Tales, Folk Tales,
Legends & Mythology—Fiction. 3. Nature & The
Environment—Fiction.
Library of Congress Control Number: 2020910380

ISBN-13: 978-1-7344833-3-8 (paperback)

On the Nature of Things

Contents

WOOD

ONCE there was a boy named John who had a sister called Margaret. They lived together at the edge of a forest in a large house that had belonged to their grandmother. Their mother cared for the house. Their father, who was in timber, paid for it. John and Margaret rarely saw their father. But they heard their mother speaking with him, frequently, on the telephone.

John and Margaret liked to eat wood. John preferred varnished, carved wood. Antique balustrades. The elegant handles of baroque tea trolleys. Margaret confined herself to living, or to spare and painted, modern wood. Hunched halfway up a birch tree, gnawing at the bark that joined branch to trunk. Pulling herself along on all fours, peeling away the lower foliage of the arbor vitae hedge. Margaret's mother's neighbors

commiserated with Margaret's mother about the local deer.

There *were* neighbors, despite the cool whisper of isolation that enveloped the house. The closest, a half mile walk along a carefully curated woodland path, sold fresh eggs to tourists when she wasn't volunteering at the local school. Valuable eggs produced by happy chickens who knew that they were loved. A brightly painted wooden duck holding a basket of pastel, wooden offspring at the end of the tastefully shabby drive indicated the prosperity of the farm. Welcoming visitors. Her husband managed a hedge fund.

A few weeks after their arrival at what had been their grandmother's house, before they'd been politely expelled from the school—private tutoring perhaps more suited to their precocious minds—John and Margaret had eaten the wooden duck. And the pastel ducklings. John had worked his way down from the tufted head, along the squat neck, to the basket, leaving a small heap of sodden paint at the carving's concrete base. Margaret had ingested the solid, smiling babies, spitting out the occasional stray bit of moss. A frown of concentrated disgust.

The next day, their neighbor had visited John's and Margaret's mother. Bright and understanding, offering compassion as well as her wealth of experience raising five raucous boys, all now settled, productive and reproductive, in the city. The day after that, two of the smugly satisfied chickens were found dead. Experimental wounds in their undersides, otherwise unmarked. Coyotes. Worse than deer. The neighbor had never returned.

But John and Margaret preferred their home to their excursions into the neighborhood. A beautiful home. A flourishing garden. A place to luxuriate in the feel, more than the taste, of the wood. The numb rub of willow, alder, and birch along the roof of the mouth. The sharp pleasure of a centuries-old splinter of colonial rocker piercing the skin between two molars. The wet component parts of a mahogany bed frame, its posters like contorted stick candy, moldering into sludge in an otherwise empty room.

At the top of the house, unusually, were the library and the music room. Great, cavernous halls that ran the length of the building. John and Margaret sampled the library daily. Digesting seventeenth-century quartos kept under glass as diligently as they consumed pulp paperbacks purchased by unnamed uncles and cousins for company in 1970s airports. The rollicking epistolary novels of confused eighteenth-century publishers to cleanse the palate in-between.

But their favorite corner of the room housed the photo albums. Layer cakes of velvet-encased board protected thick, nineteenth-century images of respectable ancestors quietly amused by their fate at the hands of their ravenous descendants. Psychedelic, mid-twentieth-century plastic volumes, barely edible, hiding, however, thin slices of reddish Polaroids taken on beaches and at

carnivals, still leaking sweet liquid when punctured by a sharp canine.

John noticed, uninterested, as he consumed the 1990s, that their mother had once been beautiful. No more. Unable to keep down food, she crept skeletally fragile about the garden. Her clothing, the sartorial flotsam of an urban profession she had abandoned to educate her children, hung awkwardly, incorrectly, from pointed and elongated shoulder blades and hips. She subsisted on the leaves of a dark greenish-purple kale plant that grew four or five feet tall on the north side of the house in the marine fog that obscured the grounds every morning, summer or winter, clouds or watery sunshine.

The kale the children left untouched. But in the spring, they ate the tulips. And the flaccid roses in the summer. The furry, orange-brown fennel, the sage, and the bee-balm. The flowers of a desperate, spinsterish blueberry bush. Every leaf of a doomed quince. A stray hummingbird, insufficiently agile, venturing a touch too close. Natural selection.

Their mother had once interplanted the tulips with larkspur and foxglove. Monkshood. Half accidentally. Wondering. When her dinner of boiled kale that evening had left her breathless, her heart hammering painful and erratic against her ribcage, she'd pulled the flowers. Her lungs still brackish, three or four days later. They didn't want her dead yet. They'd no one else to care for them. Yet.

ON THE NATURE OF THINGS

NOW, on a late spring morning in the library, John crushed the metal plate of a daguerreotype under his heel while watching his sister. She was lying curled on her side, licking the painted foot of a low bookcase. They could hear their mother pacing the room below them, muttering into the telephone. Best hear what she had to say. They'd chewed through a sustaining wall in the conservatory the night before, and three ceiling-high glass panes had slipped and shattered. She was cross.

Margaret, reading his thoughts, rose to her feet, wiping the back of her hand across her lips. John allowed himself a final satisfying grind of glass and metal under a bare, calloused toe, and held out his own hand. Clasping fingers, they left the library. Glanced into the music room at the piano. Once obsessively tuned, free of the smallest speck of dust, it was now a pale, tangled jumble of maple wood ribbons. Wires and felt rising haphazard from the wreck like the shattered bones of some long-extinct lizard.

The pyramidal metronome, however, sat pristine on a windowsill surveying the destruction. John and Margaret enjoyed the metronome. They'd spend hours gazing at motes of sawdust floating on the hot, summer air, as the metronome ticked on and on. Soothing.

Pausing at the door, John released his sister's fingers, crossed the room, and activated the metronome. Then, skirting a stray wire, he returned to Margaret and clutched her fingers once more. Brought the bitten nails to his face and inhaled her musky, mouse-like scent. After which, they approached the building's central stairway, descended to the gallery, and observed their mother's rage.

"...not overreacting. The south wing of the house is gone. Demolished. I'm frightened—" More pacing. Sniffling. "I'll make this as clear as I can. If you don't return and do something about it, I'm calling—" Whimpering. "Good. Thank you. Tomorrow, then."

She switched off the phone and looked up at the gallery. She couldn't see them, but they knew she knew they were there. After a long minute, the children withdrew once more to the top of the house. Barefoot. Red-cheeked. Blond and hungry. Planning.

THE next evening, their father returned. John and Margaret adored their father. Weak, absent, and doting. When he saw them waiting at the door, twined in one another's arms, he gathered them up and danced about the entrance hall. Breathing heavily. A few pounds overweight. Smelling of cold coffee, air-freshener, and the road. He lowered first John, and second Margaret, to the pock-marked, shattered, once-parquet floor. Then he pulled colorful sacks of candy and chocolate from his coat pockets. Each tied with a pretty, curled ribbon.

"For you."

Smiling, delicate, they accepted the bags. Opened them. Dutifully took the hard candy into their mouths. "Our favorite, father. Thank you."

John and Margaret had made an effort with their appearance. Though still barefoot, Margaret wore white shorts that emphasized her little girl's bottom and a purple t-shirt with puffed sleeves over a benevolent dragon. John had chosen faded blue jeans and a yellow button-down. Both smiled at their father. Both retained their white milk teeth. Both spat the candy into a corner of the room when their father had turned to hang his coat. In full view of their mother.

Their mother had also made an effort. She was ghastly. Her pink, cotton sun-dress set off the liverish pallor of her skin and the metallic yellow of her brittle, broken hair. When she stretched back her lips in what was meant to be a smile, her gums, the same yellow as her hair, were drawn high over thin, feeble teeth. A smudge of something dark purplish-green wedged, irrevocable, into the spaces between her bottom front incisors. She watched their father's back as he hung his coat, slow and deliberate.

"You're later than I expected."

"Traffic." He didn't turn.

"Dinner is ready now."

He hunched and then straightened his round, fleshy shoulders. Turned to face her. "I'll wash. Five minutes."

"Okay."

He took precisely five minutes. And once he'd returned to dinner, which he alone ate—a greasy leg of lamb, potatoes mashed with cream, and three helpings of quivering gelatin smothered in something white squirted out of a metal cannister—John and Margaret were sent to bed. Their mother and father remained in the dining room, sitting at the table, a place-holder in tatty, mass-produced marble purchased when the mahogany original had disappeared down the children's gullets. Talking in low, burdened contempt.

As John and Margaret crept down the stairs and toward the edge of the door to listen, they could see their mother, who was toying with the fibrous end of a kale leaf, push a pamphlet across the tabletop toward their father.

"What is it?" Their father was more interested in pouring a few final drops from the wine carafe into his glass, the lip of which was liberally smeared with the detritus of lamb, cream, and gelatin.

"From the school."

"I thought the school wanted nothing to do with them."

"They don't. But they're obligated to check on them."

"So?"

"It's a residential camp. Close by. Less than ten miles away. For children with—with disorders." She dropped her eyes to the shredded green fibers on her plate.

Their father drained his glass. "There's nothing wrong with them that a bit of discipline and understanding won't fix. They're bright. Intelligent. Social—"

"No one is questioning their intelligence." She forced herself to hold his look. "They've got— eating—problems—"

"No. You've got eating problems. Have you seen yourself?" She moved to interrupt, but he spoke over her. "Has it occurred to you that they're learning this behavior from you? To be honest, I'm impressed by their relative normality given the home you've provided them. They're growing children who eat what they can. I spend every day working to keep you housed—"

"If something isn't done," she said, "there won't be a house. They'll have eaten it. We can't go on like this."

"We can and will." He pushed back his chair. "I'm—"

"If they aren't under observation by the end of the week," she said, "I'll leave."

She stood, shivering under the thin, pink cotton. He stood as well.

"Bitch."

She said nothing.

"Arrange it, then. I'll take them. I want them nowhere near you in the meantime."

He left the room.

ON the morning they were meant to enter the Institute, John woke early. Before the light.

Punching out a thin circle of drywall from the corridor to settle his stomach, he crept down the stairs and through the entrance hall. Then, leaving the house, he shuffled across the shaggy lawn toward the shed, curling his toes against the clumped, wet blades of grass.

When he reached the shed, he pulled open the door, tried a meditative bite of the handle, and peered into the dark. It took him less than five minutes to unearth the object he sought: a fifteen-year-old Sat-Nav GPS device, still charged, still—after a quick investigation—linked to the satellite. Stuffing it into the front pocket of the sweatshirt he wore to sleep, he ran back to the house, back through the chipped hall, back up the ragged stairs, and into the room he shared with his sister.

Margaret was bleary and half-asleep, warm and smelling of hamsters in her bed. John closed their door, crossed to her, and crawled under the blankets beside her. Sniffed her exposed cheek, inhaling the scent of the undersides of rocks and of damp, fertile dirt. Whispered into her ear. "It will be all right. I'll get us home."

Her eyes still closed, she smiled. Twisted toward him in the bed. "I know you will."

Without answering, he took a lock of her ratted hair into his mouth. Chewed it for a few minutes before slipping back into sleep. And woke again only when their father, with a melancholy, false sparkle, knocked at their door to tell them that it was time to ready themselves for Camp.

ON THE NATURE OF THINGS

Their father maintained his animated chatter throughout the drive to the Institute's gates. A lengthy tour along winding, conscientiously rural roads that stitched together their neighborhood, and that always led them on the most meandering of journeys. This was a trek that John and Margaret would never replicate. Not backward. For, though the Institute was, as their mother had insisted, only ten miles away as the crow flies, they were lost once the car had passed the remains of the wooden duck.

But their true horror was reserved not for the Institute's location so much as for the building itself. Clean and modern, light and airy. Not a hint of dirt, not a splinter of wood in sight. Glass, metal, and stone stretched endlessly before them. And outside, in place of plantings, were tasteful glass sculptures of botanically impossible flowers donated by a popular artist who worked in the city and gave interviews to literary radio shows. Their mother had once appreciated him, before she'd forgotten the world.

John, repelled, dragged his eyes from the chrome-shiny ducts exposed along the ceiling to his sister's face. Where, with a stab of fury, he saw that her sullen complaisance, redolent of things decaying under hot, hazy sunlight, had given way to fear. Mastering himself under the gaze of the ruddy, respectable Ward nurse, however, he leaned forward, brotherly, and kissed Margaret's forehead.

"Here," he murmured into her clammy skin. "Tonight. At moonrise."

She nodded, clasped him, and allowed herself to be led to the girls' wing.

NINE hours later, gripping sweaty hands, John and Margaret were out the door and creeping beyond the floral sentries that wailed, hollow, in the moonlit summer wind. Crawling, beetle-like, toward the edge of the forest. Where, biting his bottom lip into bloody shreds, John stabbed with his right index finger at the device until it found the satellite. Vindicated, he wiped the sweat from his brow with Margaret's fingertips, which he held in his left hand, and pushed "home" with his right thumb. After which, smiling, he led them into the taller growth.

They reached the footpath to their grandmother's house as the sun was rising over their mother's swollen peonies. Both found peony flowers cloying, but they paused nonetheless to eat the pinkish, gumdrop buds before pushing through the door to the entrance hall. Immediately encountering their father, who was overjoyed to see them.

Their mother, however, emerging at the top of the stairs, wobbled at their sight, grabbed and missed the absent, obliterated bannister, and then righted herself. Stared down at the scene, cold and angry. And, before the children had even extricated themselves from their father's arms, she said: "I'll return them to the facility myself. Tomorrow morning."

Their father shot her a look of astonished distaste. "At least let them recover for a day or two. They've spent the night in the forest. Poor, brave children."

"No." She passed them and made her way to the front door. "Tomorrow morning."

John and Margaret spent the day eluding the joyful attentions of their father. Tumbled together in a forgotten linen cupboard on the second floor, eating handfuls of sawdust scooped from the inside of a stuffed rocking horse, its head dangling from the three or four threads that still attached it to its body. Planning. They weren't frightened. Only hungry.

But when night had fallen, and John crept from his bed to charge the device, he discovered that the door to their room was locked. And when, enraged, he pulled the knob from its socket with his strong milk teeth, he encountered a cabinet, metal, placed tight and firm against the door frame. They were confined. Swallowing his fear, he tested the device. A bit of battery remained. It would do. Returning to his own bed, lest Margaret feel his uncertainty, he spent the remainder of the night in thoughtful strategy.

The next morning, when their mother drove them in silence to the Institute, he continued to strategize. Watched, speculative, as she nodded an icy farewell in their direction, leaving them to the embarrassed and malleable nurse. Who responded, as John had predicted, to Margaret's waiflike longing. To his own stoicism beyond his years. To their mother's cadaverous neglect. Meaning that nine hours later, hand in hand, they were once again passing under the howling, blown-glass possibly-coreopsis, across a moonbeam, to the edge of the forest.

John punched at the device and found the satellite more quickly this time. A relief. But anxious nonetheless about the time they had left to them, he clutched Margaret's wrist more tightly than he intended and pulled his sister rapidly into the shadow of the trees. Toward home. Walked, increasingly—cautiously—confident, for close to an hour. Drawing strength from the wood. Until, at three past midnight, with a murmur of a flicker, the device went black. The battery sucked away.

John swallowed his breath and punched at the screen. Stabbed it with a fingertip. Bloodied his lower lip once again. To no avail. They had no guide. Margaret, slow and congested as was her habit, pushed her nose into his sticky t-shirt. Breathed his animal fear. "What do we do, John?"

He sat heavily on the damp, needled ground and pulled her into his lap. "We wait. When the sun rises, we'll find our way. We'll continue home then."

She nodded, her ear folded up against his chest. And though they didn't speak, they did eat the device, piece by piece, as they listened to the respiration of the forest. Best put it to good use. Help pass the time as the inky sky darkened into blackness prior to the flecks and fragments of light breaking through the canopy above.

When they stood, however, once more able to see, they realized that they were in a part of the forest they'd never encountered. No woodland trail. No tasteful, weathered signposts. No stump of a wooden duck. They were lost.

"It doesn't matter," John said, taking Margaret's fingers. "We'll find our way."

Margaret nodded, ripping up a willow sapling by the roots to masticate as she walked. She trusted John. He'd guide them to the edge of the wood.

But night fell, and they were still lost. Twisted together in the hollow of a log, they slept. Woke and ate the log. The lichen clinging to it. The emergent, uncurling ferns around it.

Four days later, they were deeper than ever into the forest. Walking in circles. Returning to the remains of the same log. The same lichen. The same bare stems of ferns.

Three days after that, John was failing. Unlike Margaret, who had long since shed her clothing and begun to move with a brutal, efficient energy, who was blooming and thriving in the wood, startling the occasional hedgehog, John was a refined boy. He needed more than ferns and alder branches to sustain him. He needed a proper meal.

On the tenth day, Margaret blinked down at her brother propped against the trunk of a cedar that leaked sap where she'd slashed the bark with her teeth. He was unable to move. His eyes closed and his forehead creased. Unhappy.

"Wait here," she said to him. "I'll find something for you."

John was too weak to reply.

Pressing her palms and the soles of her feet against the dirt of the forest floor, Margaret propelled herself in a direction they'd not explored. But she knew that what she sought was there. She could smell it on the wind. And indeed, a half hour later, it emerged from the brush. A beautiful house. A flourishing garden. All wood. Varnished and civilized.

Turning on her tail, her girlish bottom bobbing above the brambles, she brought the news to John. Pulled him to his knees. Whispered raspy encouragement into his ear as she moved him forward.

It took the remainder of the day to drag him there, but when he saw it, he smiled and brought a strand of her hair between his lips. Beholden. Cherishing his strong, rank sister.

And when night fell, they approached the exterior fence of the building with an emotion close to delirious fever. The fence was a trellis made of cherrywood that had been carved into cartoonish pinecones. And then covered with a climbing hydrangea. Boundless. Endless. Infinite-seeming. As they drew near, they were close to weeping.

Rather than weeping, however, they ate the not-quite-infinite trellis. The far-from-boundless

16

pinecones. And the smallish, after all, clump of hydrangea that had tumbled to the ground in the absence of support. Still hungry, they were on the verge of creeping closer, to sample the front porch, when a sound from the house sent them scuttling back beyond the perimeter of the forest. Rejuvenated, they could now bide their time.

The next night, they ate the porch. Most of the porch. A riot of brightly painted oak shaped and bent into the frailest of lattices, overlaying a thick, pungent slab of hardwood. Gluttonous, they chewed through the tight grain of the slab, stopping only when the footsteps behind the door came to an abrupt halt, and the knob began to turn.

The night after, they finished off the porch. But before they could make their way to the shingles of lignum vitae overhanging a basket of bright white pelargonium that decorated a window to the side, the door swung open. Standing backlit against a warm interior, pulsating with the scent of acacia and pine, was a woman. Thin. Confident. Wearing a dressing gown. Smiling a witch's smile.

"You poor children. Are you hungry? There's more to eat inside." The woman opened the door wider, allowing John and Margaret a view of the golden interior. A darkly shimmering bannister. A workshop of carved giants and trolls, goblins and gnomes, all of wood, all visible just beyond.

Mesmerized, John and Margaret entered the house. The door closed behind them. The scent of wood swelled.

"This way, children." The woman led them toward the kitchen.

John, however, having regained his strength and his acumen, knew better than to let the story spool out to its inevitable conclusion. Long before the woman had brought them to the end of the corridor, he had sprung at her, sinking his teeth into her spine. Margaret, joining him, leapt at the throat. And, together, they waited for the woman to crumple to the pinewood floor. Extinguished.

When they were certain that the witch was dead, they rose to their feet, licking blood off their noses and chins.

"What now?" asked Margaret.

"The stove?" John supposed tradition was best. He began to remove the dressing gown, the better to stuff the body into the small, modern oven that they could just make out beyond the kitchen door.

But as he searched for a place to store the dressing gown, the wail of an infant floated down from some upper bedroom. Dislodging a memory. Long calloused over.

John blinked down at the thin, dead woman's thin, naked breast. A bubble of something clear and white leaked and dripped from its side. Still thinking, still remembering, he flicked her blood from his upper lip with the tip of his tongue. Recalled once, before time, biting down on another breast, another woman, her flinching gasp, the rush of milk mingled with blood. Almost better than wood. Certainly better than dirt.

He raised his eyes to his sister's and saw that she too was remembering. "Wait," he said. "I've got a better idea."

Margaret dropped the ankle she was holding. "What?"

"First," he said, holding up the dressing gown, "I'll sort this. And then," frowning at the cries that were growing in intensity upstairs, "I'll take care of that. And only *then*," he concluded, "will we dispose of the witch. And the wood. We'll share."

Margaret sat naked in the pool of blood on the floor. Toyed with the witch's splayed fingers. Wondered how keratin compared to willow bark. "Okay," she replied. "I'll wait here."

SILK

ROSE and Frances, aging sisters, disliked one another. Every week, on the Thursday, they lunched together at a local restaurant, meeting upon Rose's return from visiting her eldest son, the estate attorney with the musically gifted daughter. Frances had no children of her own, and Rose enjoyed pitying Frances on these occasions. On this Thursday, however, she was feeling more sorry for herself than for her sister. Perturbed by the aggressive behavior of the neighbor children, alone with their father now that their mother had slipped into that bulimia-induced coma.

As Rose cut the motor of her Subaru in the drive of the restaurant, she looked sidelong at Frances, uncertain whether to unburden herself. Unwilling to cede emotional territory. Unhappy admitting a crack in the unblemished domesticity that she cultivated against her sister's rented bungalow and solitary, pre-packaged life. Her decision was made for her—keep mum—when Frances, pulling herself from the car, stumbled across an odd little man who had appeared at the extreme edge of the restaurant's embowered entryway.

He'd surely not been there when Rose had backed the Subaru into the spot beside the variegated holly. And he certainly didn't belong. The restaurant, a farmhouse, occupied a position of splendid retreat at the far end of a meadow, serving food cultivated on-site in its kitchen gardens or locally sourced from emotionally fulfilled suppliers. Its proprietors bought eggs from Rose every Saturday in preparation for their famous brunch. And their sign at the end of the drive referenced, with quiet wit, the goats whose milk produced their bespoke, limited-run cheese. It was a rural, clean, and friendly business.

The man slouching unsteady on the fringe of the farmhouse's crumbled granite stoop was neither clean nor friendly. He belonged on the pavement of an urban convenience store. The sort of place from which Rose's eldest son bought cigarettes on the sly when he believed he was alone. Elsewhere.

Nonetheless, Frances should have known better than to halt, startled and blinking, on the margin of the first step. Telegraphing her unease. Rose pressed her lips together as she watched her sister's hesitation. Then she mounted the porch

21

herself and nodded a pleasant greeting to the man. Pulled Frances along behind her as she passed.

"Pat the dog?"

They both stopped. The man, they noted as they turned, though small and dry, was not old. His matted hair and beard were glossy. His teeth, though brown and stinking, were strong. His hands lithe under the dirt. And his eyes were bright. Contemptuous. Amused.

The dog, as though in deliberate counterpoint to the man, was wretched. At best, it could have been ill. At worst, it was—something else. It may once have been a Labrador. Its color perhaps yellow. But the fur along its back and sides was rubbed mostly away. Its claws chipped. Something viscid dripped from one eye. And its stench was staggering, ominous because it failed to register as "dog" at all. The creature smelled of unwashed, rotting, and yet unquestionably human body parts. Feet. A groin. Places best left unexplored.

"I love dogs. Isn't he a darling?" Rose knelt. Undaunted. Not to be cowed.

"She." The man gazed down at Rose squatting before the stinking Lab.

"*Isn't* she a darling?" Rose pressed her face against the dog's muzzle and allowed it to run its pinkish-grey tongue across her cheek and nose. The stench grew, rising in waves from the dog's black gums. Yet Rose continued, unfaltering.

Frances, less stalwart, pressed a weak hand against the restaurant's closed door and watched, sickened, as the scene unfolded. The dog, which wore a lead of knotted, multicolored cotton handkerchiefs, seemed to her less a separate organism than a pseudopod extension of the man. An additional limb. Another body part, touching passers by who would be hesitant to "pat" the man himself. She wondered, vaguely, whether Rose would have submitted so readily to the man, to any man, licking her face, rubbing his long, canine fingernails over her hands and shoulders. Where her sister's vanity ended.

But the thought was cut short when Rose, having proved her point, straightened, pulling a wet-wipe from her handbag. "Lovely, brave animal," she said, cleaning the pus-like saliva from her face and fingers.

The man, ignoring her, turned to Frances. "Pat the dog?"

Frances swallowed. Shook her head in the negative. Dropped her eyes to the creeping thyme that sprouted through the cracks of the restaurant's stone porch.

The man pursed his lips. Flicked his gaze to Rose. "Great wealth." Then he turned his attention back to Frances and considered her downcast expression. "Silence."

Frances turned without raising her eyes to his. Uninterested in whether the man's words were a description or a prediction. Either way, they left her demoralized. She also refused to look up at the small, satisfied smile Rose wore as she swept into the restaurant to take up their usual table.

ROSE always ate sensibly. Though she kept active and wore clothing that could take her easily from Pilates studio to art gallery, nothing tight or tailored, she knew better than to tempt fate by gorging herself. She also took pleasure in watching her sister's weekly failure to emulate her diet. As she stabbed a small, blue borage flower and pale, white viola onto her salad fork, she pushed down a second smile at the empty bowl of gruyere mac and cheese Frances had emptied five minutes earlier. Wondered how long it would take before the inevitable request for the dessert menu came.

Tilting her head, she considered the restaurant's current greens offering spread out before her. In addition to the borage and viola flowers, she recognized calendula petals, sorrel, dandelion greens, clover, and wild arugula. Food to gather by the roadside. Odd that it should cost her sister three days' rent. If Frances ever paid for it, that is. Rose was also looking forward to her sister's pained offer to cover the bill, invariably refused.

Or, perhaps, not refused this time. The encounter with the dog had left Rose unsettled. Craving a bit of cruelty. She lifted a pale, immature slug from under a wide arugula leaf with the tip of her fork and left it curled at the side of her unused bread plate. Proof of the restaurant's no-toxins policy.

Eight or nine seconds later, a healthy, furry server, looking like a tattooed bear dressed as a truck-driver or pantomime lumberjack, passed the

24

table and tipped the slug into a bucket of beer he carried for that purpose. "No extra protein today, then?" Jovial.

"Watching my weight." Rose smiled up at him. It was an ongoing joke.

He laughed and continued to the next table to explain to a party of newcomers the process by which the restaurant produced its on-site sausages.

As Rose resumed her inspection of the salad, toying with the notion of allowing Frances to buy their lunch, she felt something lodge itself in her throat. Nothing dangerous. She could breathe. But some bit of—material—was entrenched in the insubstantial, half-imagined space between esophagus and diaphragm.

She swallowed and cleared her throat. Felt the object move, horribly, up rather than down. Drank off the remainder of her whisky (no white wine; she was anything but a cliché). The thing came further up, almost into her mouth. She tasted bile. And paper? Moved to signal to her sister. But then she noticed Frances's state.

Red-faced, her eyes watering, Frances was coughing phlegm into a handkerchief. Heaving, shuddering, loud and out of control, she was also drawing the embarrassed attention of neighboring patrons. It was only minutes later that she regained control of her breathing and dropped her face into the crook of her elbow. Overturning a water glass.

Rose, still delicately hacking, but hiding it better than Frances had, extended a graceful arm across the empty plates, exquisite wrist catching the light, and patted Frances's hot, trembling shoulder two or three times. Annoyed rather than concerned. Then she withdrew her hand and coughed. Quietly.

Frances raised her head from her arm. Stared, dull-eyed, at Rose. But she wasn't so spent that she left the ruined handkerchief in view. Mortified by what she'd deposited into it, she stuffed it into the pocket of the shapeless coat she'd hung over the back of her chair. Rose registered, beneath her polite disgust, that the handkerchief was shiny—stiff and sticky—rather than wet or spent as she'd have expected it to be. But she didn't dwell on the anomaly. Frances was incurable regardless of the state of her handkerchief.

"What happened?"

"I don't—" Frances cut short her explanation and stared down at the table.

Crouching between them, in the center of the cheerfully floral tablecloth, was a tiny, jewel-green frog. Oversized, ruby-red eyes. Splayed, tangerine-orange toes. Striped, turquoise-blue belly. It was looking, quizzical, up at Frances.

"Is it real?" Frances moved a tentative fingertip in its direction. It cocked its head, but otherwise it didn't move.

"It must have come from my salad."

"What?" Frances shifted her attention from the frog to her sister.

"My salad." Rose was still trying to dislodge the matter from the back of her throat without

26

making the scene her sister had. Uninterested in the addition to the table.

"More unwanted protein?" The bear with the bucket of beer had returned.

"Yes." Rose had brought her napkin from her lap and was coughing demurely into its deep folds. She didn't look up at him.

"You sure you don't—" He stopped, peering down at the frog. Frances, obscurely protective, had spread her own fingers over it. He raised his eyebrows. "It's a red-eyed treefrog. From Costa Rica. You shouldn't have brought it here. Against code."

"It isn't mine," Frances replied. Lame-sounding even to herself.

"I've told you," Rose said, gazing into the depths of her napkin, her cough now gone, "it came from my salad."

"I don't think so," the bear said. "Not local." Then he turned back to Frances. "It'll catch a chill if you don't get it to a terrarium."

When Frances said nothing, and Rose, also silent, began prodding at her napkin with a queasy, inquisitive fingernail, he nodded once, curt. "Look. We'll give you a brandy glass for now to take it home. Bring it back next time you're here."

"But—" Frances caught herself again. Silent, she nodded.

When the bear returned, he tipped the frog, docile and compliant, into the snifter, which he handed in turn to Frances. Frances, obedient, wrapped it in her coat, thinking to keep it warm.

Then she turned to Rose, steeling herself to make her customary, humiliating offer to pay their bill.

But before she could get the words out, Rose shook her head. "My turn."

After which, to the unconcealed revulsion of the bear, Rose reached into her filthy napkin and drew out a vile, dripping wad of grubby twenty-dollar notes. A good eighteen or nineteen of them. She shoved the wet cash into his hand, told him to keep the change, and beckoned Frances to follow her. "I must have brought more than I thought."

Frances, glancing behind her at the bear, who had shoved the money into a pocket before wiping his hands on his plaid shirt, stumbled once again, held her coat and brandy-snifter tightly, and followed her sister out the door.

THE next afternoon, Frances drove alone to the pet-supply shop in the city to purchase a terrarium. Three terraria. One for frogs, one for snakes, and one for assorted arthropods. Assembling a collection. For though it was true that most of the fauna she regurgitated were, despite the bear, local—small brown toads, ungainly house spiders on teetering legs, and muted, olive garter snakes that were content to hop, creep, or slither into the overgrown crab grass skirting the unaesthetic concrete slab beneath her bungalow's aluminum back door—others plainly were not.

The more colorful, threatening, or unusual specimens she kept warm in the brandy-snifter until she could identify them and move them to a proper container. Pleased by, rather than ashamed of, the library of nineteenth- and twentieth-century volumes of natural history that she'd hoarded in her capacity as copy-editor for a failing geographical society's journal. Deficiently bound books stacked horizontally not only on sagging shelves, but also on the unstable chairs scattered throughout the bungalow, chairs that Frances had extracted in pieces from mail-order boxes and fitted together with hex keys and spare bolts.

Rose had always mocked the ugly books both for their politics—inescapably colonial—and for their inaccuracies—why not Wikipedia? She'd scorned to mention the chairs. But Frances enjoyed the feel, the linear process, that accompanied turning brittle pages in search of some relevant, or irrelevant, bit of wisdom. And now, she could find what she needed without drawing the attention of curious online algorithms out to sell her a cure. A cure she wasn't certain, if she was honest with herself, that she wanted.

She'd already deduced that the vermin—or so she supposed she must call them—materialized with more frequency when she spoke and when she ate. Chattering to herself in the kitchen as she'd spooned up peanut butter from a jar had produced a maelstrom of serpents and amphibious life, all the more distressing because the former had quickly begun to ingest the latter. A slaughter.

Frances had dropped, repentant, to her knees on the salmon-colored linoleum and gathered up the snakes into her snifter, shooing the frogs and occasional newt into the wet dusk outdoors. Having sorted the snakes, she'd then carefully washed her hands, found her overcoat, and sought out the overstuffed chair with the crocheted antimacassar—the only piece of furniture in the house she valued—to think. Because she'd also deduced that the animals, though demanding, were a distraction rather than the answer to her condition.

The handkerchief was the answer.

In the waning light, Frances had withdrawn the wadded piece of cloth from her coat pocket. Forced herself to examine it as she'd lacked the courage to do before. And what she saw had convinced her.

The handkerchief had been a commonplace square of dyed green cotton that she'd received free in a box of tulip bulbs that had failed to sprout the previous spring. Cheap and ugly. Spraying it with what she'd thought at the time was a gristly specimen of respiratory mucus, however, had transformed it into a piece of incandescent silk. Thick silk. The sort of silk she'd seen displayed behind layers of glass, under muted golden lights, in the city's museum.

Or, squinting at it more closely, not transformed it. Overlaid it. The silk threads interlocked minutely across the handkerchief's coarse cotton surface, producing a three-dimensional lace-like effect. Intuitively, Frances knew that these threads were spider- rather than caterpillar-silk. This was not the sort of textile one plucked, however daintily, from a mulberry bush.

But how was she producing it? Not when she spoke or ate, certainly. Two or three experiments and a brandy snifter-full of aquatic African frogs had convinced her of that. The silk, unlike the vermin, came involuntarily. Unannounced. In the restaurant, it had bubbled up only as she'd silently hummed to herself to avoid internalizing Rose's pity.

Hummed to herself. Reclining in the chair, the room nearly dark, Frances had considered. Then, half-ashamed, she'd whispered a toneless few bars of a nursery rhyme. Before bending forward, violently double, and hacking something wet and impossibly light into her hand. Reaching out above her head with her other hand to switch on a standing lamp, she'd uncurled her fingers. In her palm was an unmatched tangle of fine, damp thread.

The next morning, Frances had woken to discover another small mound of silver thread beside her pillow. One sticky end still adhering to the dry, cracked corner of her mouth. Did she talk in her in her sleep? Hum? It didn't matter. She'd disengaged the material from her lip, scooped it up with her fingertips, and deposited it into an empty sewing box inherited from her mother. The one Rose hadn't wanted.

She'd then eaten little and spoken not at all once she'd entered the city—uncertain she'd be competent to explain the odd scorpion or salamander escaping her vigilance and disappearing into the corridors of the pet-supply shop. But she'd felt happier than she had for a long time. Looking forward to her return. To the books, to the serpents, and to the silk.

When she'd reached her house that evening, she'd silently roamed her cramped living room, pulling volumes off shelves and from under chairs. Having retrieved what she wanted, she had then settled into her overstuffed chair with a heavy book in her lap and a mug of hibiscus tea to her side. Heaved open the book. Now, hours later, she was still in the chair.

"The apparatus," she read in a treatise on the structure of spiders published in 1830, "by which spiders construct their ingenious fabrics is much more complicated than that which we have described as common to the various species of caterpillars. Caterpillars have only two reservoirs for the materials of their silk; but spiders, according to the dissections of M. Treviranus, have four principal vessels." She ran her tongue along the inside of her mouth and cheeks, seeking evidence of glands or reservoirs. Found nothing.

She paged ahead and continued reading. "We have seen that the silken thread of a caterpillar is composed of two united within the tube of the spinneret, but the spider's thread would appear, from the first view of its five spinnerets to be quintuple, and in some species which have six teats, so many times more." She closed the volume and frowned. Tried to feel for deeper changes to her body. Beyond her mouth. Anything to indicate the internal "teats" that might be filling, prepared to flow out and through her throat. Too obvious, perhaps.

And so, she picked up a newer study and read further. "Spider silk is unmatched in its combined tensile strength and ductility." Felt a tiny prick of pride. A bit like Rose. Perused an entertaining treatise on the military applications of dragline and capture silk, which could, according to the slightly breathless author, surpass Kevlar in its absorption of energy. It was already used for the crosshairs on the army's optical lenses. Why not flak-jackets as well? Closed the book. Considered again. Decided to avoid the military as much as possible in the coming weeks.

And then, careful and deliberate, she cleared her throat. Hummed a few bars from Debussy. Took up the pale threads she'd spat into her lap and spread them between her fingers. Cat's Cradle. Admired the luminous, dew-soaked strands that moved according to physical laws all their own in the inferior light of her standing lamp. Felt her pride grow.

After that, chastising herself, she coiled the silk, reached down to a quilted bag she kept beside her chair and, feeling about inside, drew up a crochet hook. Licked her finger to begin work. Continued humming.

THE next Thursday, Rose and Frances met again for lunch. Rose, however, couldn't stay long because she had an emergency appointment at the dentist's. And Frances, once they were seated at their usual table, understood why. Though she tried to cover it, Rose had chipped away the bottom edges of both of her front teeth. Where once careful orthodontia had conjured into existence a perfect, if understated, smile, now only jagged white nubs remained. Frances looked a question at her sister as she indicated to the bear that she'd want nothing more than a glass of mineral water today.

"An accident," Rose explained. "Clive wants me talking. And the more I talk, the more—oh shit, wait a second." She reached under her chair for a capacious, mass-produced leatherette handbag, wrenched it open, and heaved into it something that sounded like rocks wrapped in paper. When she'd finished, she peered inside, rummaged about with her hand, and pulled out three or four gleaming red stones. Sniffed, disappointed, and tossed them back. "Spinel. Worthless."

Clive was Rose's husband. Frances looked sympathetic, but she didn't speak. Sipped her water.

"Don't give me that look." Rose beckoned to the bear. "I feel fortunate that he's still interested in what I have to say after all these years. Though you wouldn't understand, obviously. Most marriages—the three-cheese moose-meat lasagna and a rum and coke, please." This to the bear.

Rose looked larger as she inhabited her seat. Capacious like her handbag. Frances was about to

34

risk a compliment on the change, but she closed her mouth when Rose, taken by surprise, vomited copiously onto the tablecloth. Wracked, but unperturbed. When she'd finished, she'd produced a damp clump of hundred-dollar bills, five uncut diamonds, and what looked to Frances like, perhaps, stock certificates? Frowning, Rose, swept it all into the bag. And it was a bag. Functional. Nothing more. Rose no longer concerned herself with tasteful accessories.

"Are you all right?" Frances coughed quietly and brought up pair of delicate reddish-silver children's gloves. Gossamer soft. Set them beside her empty plate.

The bear, who was returning to clean the non-monetary detritus that Rose had deposited on the tablecloth, paused to examine the gloves. "May I?"

Frances nodded.

The bear held the fabric up to the blue light falling through the window. Gently, he replaced them. "They're beautiful. I've never seen a red like that."

Frances smiled. She'd been practicing with color. And then, remembering, she raised a finger. Reached into her own functional handbag and found his brandy snifter. Handed it to him. "Thank you."

A tiny, brown spider on her tongue. She turned to the side to spit it into her hand and let it lower itself to the ground. The key was self-control.

"No worries." The bear was still fascinated by the gloves. He hadn't noticed the spider.

Rose, however, had. Narrowing her eyes, she stood. "I'll be late for the dentist. You pay this time, dear."

She left before Frances had the chance to reply. Frances reached once again for her bag.

But the bear stopped her. "Nothing to pay for. You haven't eaten."

Frances nodded, left the gloves on the table, and returned home.

OVER the next weeks, Frances immersed herself in research on spider silk. She learned that though aqueous in the body, the material dries hard upon exposure to air. She learned about spidroin 1 and spidroin 2, the proteins that compose dragline silk. She learned about glycine and alanine, the amino acids of which spider silk is composed. "Crystalline alanine," unique in the world. She muttered the words to herself as she spat out little heaps of knotted glitter. Along with the occasional, sticky, surprised toad.

But she also turned her attention to glutamine, serine, leucine, valine, and proline, the lesser amino acids that her invisible glands were secreting. She thought, now, that she could feel her "teats" working. Deep in her chest. Leaving her mind clean, pure, and serene. Some hormone, no doubt. Dehumanizing her. She didn't mind. Nothing could shame her as she spun. As she built.

Webs and cocoons for her animals. Steel-strong structures—furniture, dolls' houses, candelabra, a bookcase—that billowed out, invincible, on the slenderest current of air. Gloves, stockings, hats, and shoes that stretched into automobiles, boats, or train carriages before shrinking, undamaged, into their original state. A flak-jacket in pale pink. For the breathless soldier. And, she eventually decided, a tunic of molecule-thin, golden silk for Rose. Rose, who was sadly altered.

The sisters no longer met at the restaurant on the edge of the meadow because Rose never left her house. Instead, every Thursday, Frances rode a silver bicycle down the woodland path, past the concrete stump where the wooden duck had once stood, and up to the be-jeweled door of Rose's palatial residence. No more eggs. Selling eggs was beneath her station.

Once there, Frances left the bicycle beneath a hastily constructed web of camouflage—no use tempting the feral neighbor children—and entered the house. Mounted the grand stairway bedecked with the East Asian art objects that Clive had taken to accumulating at Sotheby's sales, and made her way to Rose's hot and solitary bower.

There, with infinite stealth, she settled herself on the small stool at the edge of Rose's bed. Asked after her sister's health. Spat out a slim black viper. Expecting no answer. For Rose, as always, was eating. A mountain of toothless flesh beneath a coverlet of lumpy cashmere, she gorged herself on bright pink spheres of synthetic sugar coated in artificial white coconut and ripped from transparent plastic wrappings, insects of all kinds re-imagined in gummy gelatin, a bowl of greenish cream flecked with waxy chocolate, and bar after bar after bar of what the packages claimed were "mounds." Pausing in her feeding only periodically, every two or three minutes, to spew out hillocks of precious stones, metal ingots, and chunk after chunk of wrapped cash.

Sneering, Rose noticed her repentant, less fortunate sister sitting beside her. Bit the head from an off-season Easter rabbit molded of dry, aging chocolate. "Go find Clive. I'm hungry."

Frances nodded, silent, and left the tunic behind her on the chair. Went in search of Rose's husband. Somewhere in the house. Clive no longer managed the hedge fund. Now, so far as Frances understood, he managed Rose.

GRAIN

WHAT'S it made of?" Arthur squeezed the wrinkly, blue shoulder of the repellent little sculpture. Squeamish and fascinated. The material left a residue of powder on his fingertips. He fought down the urge to sniff his hand.

"A special kind of leather." The shopkeeper was as repellent as his wares.

But Arthur had expected that. Sought him out. Made a dedicated journey to the city, closing the restaurant for the day, when he'd learned that the workshop was granting a rare open-morning. Ordinarily, patrons bought the shopkeeper's work sight unseen. But Arthur's objective demanded a visit. He didn't want to purchase the thing without visiting it in person.

"Goat skin and wood?" He squatted in front of the sculpture and peered at its twisted, extravagantly Scandinavian features. A girl-thing. In torment. A little less than five feet tall.

"Something like that." Dismissive. The shopkeeper licked his thin, crude lips in the direction of Arthur's fiancée, who was hovering halfway out the door. Appreciating her inability to breathe inside. The place reeked like a tannery.

Arthur forced himself to look away from the sculpture's bulging inky eyes and blinked, surprised, in her direction. His fiancée, short, solid, and pragmatic, was neither the type to wilt under a bad smell nor the sort to draw the lascivious attention of chance strangers. Then he dropped his gaze back to his prospective purchase. Didn't want Hannah to pounce on his divided attention as an opportunity to suggest they leave.

As he examined the etched detail of the sculpted girl's frayed and plaited hair, he rubbed the six-inch tattoo of the Aztec God of Healing that decorated his lower left calf. Just beneath the shredded hem of his cargo shorts. Rubbed it a bit harder with his calloused thumb. Then, giving in, he picked at the scabby tissue with a fingernail and flicked a fair sized piece of it down toward the sculpture's narrow, elegant shoes. He'd commissioned the tattoo when he'd decided to marry Hannah three weeks before. After a great deal of ambivalence. It still hurt.

He risked a glance toward the door. She'd left. Waiting on the pavement. Good. More time to examine the art-thing in front of him. He placed his large palms on either side of its scuffed, sculpted winter coat and lifted it. Remarkably light. Twisted it backward. Fought down the brief, irrational impression that it was looking at him, its eyes turned inward, through its skull, beyond its disheveled hair. Angry and confused. Contemplated the Hannah problem once again.

Hannah was a problem, rather than simply Hannah, because Arthur knew that he had bad luck with relationships. The one before Hannah, the beautiful one, had decided after three years that she preferred women to furry, tattooed men who cooked well. She'd then taken herself off to some flat, agricultural region to raise soybeans with another of Arthur's former girlfriends. And the one before that, the intelligent one, had decided that she preferred cats. Disappearing without a word one star-smeared night along with Thor, the semi-feral Canada lynx that used to push itself up against the restaurant's glass doors on winter nights. Arthur missed the lynx.

Hannah was neither beautiful nor intelligent. She did, though, earn a healthy income, which helped more than Arthur liked to admit in supporting the kitchen gardens, the limited-run goat cheese, the apiary, the cottage-sausage industry, and now, the unusually vigorous, possibly mutant, hops bines that would cement his position as the pre-eminent independent brewer in the county. He pushed his index finger against the sculpture's squat nose and felt the life-like drop of wood-leather mucus that hung from it. Watched the thing wobble. He liked it, he decided. He'd take it.

"It looks like that girl who disappeared a few years ago. Creepy."

Arthur tensed. He hadn't heard Hannah return to the shop. "What girl?"

"The one from the news." Hannah bent over and examined the thing's face. "Inge. Ingrid. Something. You remember. She was—mature. Used to display herself more than was good for a girl that age. They found all those scraps of her clothing around the swamp beyond the Institute. No body. Everyone assumed she'd been, um, interfered with." She straightened. "It's horrible, Arthur. Leave it, and let's find something that won't drive away your customers."

"They aren't customers," he muttered, "they're guests." Then, lifting the sculpture by its slender waist, which, oddly, he could feel beneath the hard winter coat—as though it had been constructed, first, and deliberately, to be sculpted over—he made his way to the shopkeeper's register. "And I don't remember any girl. I don't read trash news."

Hannah smiled as she followed him. She enjoyed Arthur's touchy purity. Liked to think that it kept her clean as well. Nonetheless, she made a last effort. "Really, Arthur. You think the old ladies who pay you eighty dollars per plate to eat pansies and dandelions will find that thing appealing?"

"The old ladies," he said, "eat upstairs. This is for below. The brewery. The Liquid Loaf. I don't want to spend the rest of my life catering to disappointed housewives. The younger generation will respond to this."

Hannah knew better than to argue. Biting back a remark on the sort of response he'd likely solicit, she sought out the fresh air of the street. Frowned at a trickle of toxic, burning sludge that seeped from a crack in the shop's foundations. It was odd how infrequently the place opened. Surfaced. As though every other day of the year it was lurking, subterranean, waiting for a peculiar, unwholesome, and special sort of interest. She crossed her arms, shivering in the heat, impatient for their return to the hygienic meadow.

ARTHUR spent three anxious days moving the horrid sculpture from spot to spot in the restaurant's cellar. Whenever he thought he'd found the ideal position, the girl-thing would shrink, melting into the shadows as though ashamed of its prominence. And it was only the morning before The Liquid Loaf's grand opening that he hit upon a solution, investing in a spotlight and shoving the sculpture onto a dais. There, brightly lit, the vermin that peeked from the plaited hair and from the full, childish lips parted in an involuntary "o" were thrown into sharp relief. Nordic Gothic. Precisely the effect he was seeking.

As he brought his hand away from the sculpted knee with its sloppy, wooden-woolen sock—feeling an unexpected reluctance to sever contact with it—an inert wingless fly fell from the object's hat. Frustrated, Arthur crumbled the thing into powder between his thumb and index finger. There were too many of them anyway. A miscalculation on the part of the shopkeeper. Throughout the remainder of the day, Arthur's fingers smelled of leather rot. And, faintly, of yeast. Preoccupied by the opening, he failed to notice.

But the opening was all that he had hoped it would be. The Liquid Loaf, a moody, underground cavern overhung by a disreputable fug of recently legal narcotics and thickly twined hops bines that flourished under UV lamps, proved to be the ideal counterpoint to the restaurant above. Perfect foil for the floral wallpaper, the whimsical, elfin lighting fixtures, and the crudely charming, hand-made candles. A dark place for the cynical children of the women who ate marigolds upstairs. People enjoyed themselves.

The hops bines, it's true, were perhaps a touch prominent. Difficult to control as they throve on the acrid smoke curling over the tables. But they paled in comparison to the sculpture of the girl-thing raised on its pedestal. Broadcasting the smell of yeast—inappropriate, the wrong smell for a little girl—ever more insistently as the evening wore on. More pronounced even than the smell of beer.

But, despite the smell, *everyone,* Arthur was pleased to note, admired her. Or—perhaps— "admired" was the wrong word. Though they tried as far as possible to hide from him the discomfort that her shocking Scandinavian expression elicited, there came a time when they could no longer keep quiet. And Arthur himself couldn't help but overhear them, as the beer and smoke did their work, as conversations grew less guarded.

"...you know, the one who disappeared in the swamp last year. I'm not saying it was her fault. She was a child. Twelve or thirteen. But it was complicated. That teacher had already lost his job the year before—"

"He denied it—"

"That's what I'm saying. It was complicated. The girl wasn't right. Low self-esteem, or something. She—cultivated—the wrong kind of attention. Not that it was her fault. I'm not saying that. Obviously, I wouldn't say that—"

"Didn't they make an arrest early on once she'd disappeared? Not the teacher. The other one. That logging millionaire with the two kids. His wife died a few months ago?"

"Vegetative. Not dead."

"I'd be vegetative too if my husband liked twelve-year-olds."

"They let him go. No evidence. And he wasn't the only one. Once they looked into it, they linked that girl to half the men in the county. She wasn't—"

"You know?" Slurred and intoxicated. "All of this is making me want to find that video she posted online. A month or two before she disappeared? With the shoes? *Where* did a girl like that find those shoes—"

"You're drunk. That's gross. She was *twelve*."

"Thirteen. And she was a big girl for thirteen. Look at that sculpture. You can see it even under the coat—"

"Posting porn on the internet doesn't legitimize kidnapping, rape, and murder—"

"It wasn't porn. If it had been, they'd have removed it. Look, I'll find it for you now." Rummaging for a phone. "It was just the shoes—"

"And besides, no one knows *what* happened. She vanished. Bits of her clothing tossed about the swamp. Could be she decided to take off to the city. Wider hunting ground, right?"

"The more I look at it, the more I think that sculpture is unpleasantly accurate. At first, it seems exaggerated. Fantastic. Like a cartoon. But then it grows on you. Like it's listening. God, are those tears? Is it crying?"

"Now who's drunk?" An overturned glass. "And she's not crying, she's *angry*. Pouty. A bad little girl—"

Arthur, unable to bear it any longer, closed the brewery an hour early. Just past midnight. Content with the success of the opening. Then, mechanically accepting their congratulations, he shooed the stumbling patrons out the door, extinguished all but the spotlight, and moved a chair to the dais to gaze up at his sculpture. It wasn't crying. It wasn't angry. It was made of wood and leather. The tears were a trick of the lamps.

46

ON THE NATURE OF THINGS

HANNAH found him five hours later, as the summer dawn was turning the meadow orange. His head rested on the girl-thing's shoes, which were in turn tied down, via thick, sculpted ropes of silk, to a lumpy bread-like pedestal. One huge hand was clasped around its frail ankle. Above the shoes. The smell of yeast still lingered in the air. And the hops bine had grown three or four feet up the stone stairway leading to the surface.

"It went well, I think." Hannah, narrow-eyed, was looking at his fingers clutching the slim ankle.

Arthur, his head pounding, squinted up at her. Reluctantly, he moved his hand. "Yes. Better than I'd hoped. I'm pleased."

"You'll check on the goats this morning? Or shall I do it?"

He stood and rolled back his shoulders. Ran three fingers through his beard, which was disarranged. A bit rank. "Would you, Hannah? I'm not sure I'm up to it today." He paused, uncertain. Then, rushing forward, he spoke again. Tripping over the words. "Does she seem unhappy up there, do you think? On the pedestal? I can take her down. Cover her up a little more. Keep her in the shadows."

"She?"

"It." He cleared his throat. "You know. 'It.' The sculpture. Shall I move it again?"

"It's perfect where it is, Arthur." Flat voice. "Quite the hit last night. Certainly proved me wrong, didn't it?"

Arthur found himself flushing under his beard. He felt he had something to hide, but he couldn't think what it was. Then, steadying himself: "I'll stay here for now. Clean the place up."

"You do that, Arthur." She turned and retreated toward the surface and the daylight.

Arthur waited for the sound of the door shutting, and then he lowered himself once more to the chair at the base of the pedestal. Switched on the spotlight. Stared, intent, at the harassed features of the sculpture. It looked more beleaguered than angry or humiliated this morning. Tired, exhausted, unable or unwilling to persevere. Yet, there it stood. Enduring.

As he gazed at it, a large black beetle—living, not one of the shopkeeper's details—fell from a broad leaf of the hops bine to the girl-thing's wooden-woolen hat. It clung to the thick, scored material with clacking pincers for a second or two, and then it began to explore its new environment. First, it crept from the edge of the hat to the plaited hair. From the hair, it scuttled to the thing's chin and paused, finding its bearings, before crawling, slow and intrigued, over the full, open lips, across the hint of wet teeth. Extended a sharp, black antenna into a nostril. Paused again, interested.

Then, losing its footing, it tumbled into an opening in the sculpted overcoat. Arthur lost sight of it for close to a minute while it presumably sought a way out from under the immobile girl-thing's clothing. Dragging itself over her exposed skin, in the dark, beneath the wooden wool. Eventually, it emerged near the bottom hem of the coat, where it grasped the edge of the short skirt with its pincers. Pulled itself up and under. Disappeared once more. Arthur closed his eyes.

When he opened them, the beetle had reappeared. It was visible now at the top of the wrinkled knee-sock. Climbing down toward the ankle. Over the elegant shoes. Onto the uneven bread-like lump. The sculpture seemed to Arthur to shudder. Emitting its faint yeast-scent.

Arthur lifted the beetle, dropped it to the floor, and crushed it with the heel of his boot.

Then, hating himself, he wiped the bits of black carapace onto the flagstones and fled up the stairs. To the meadow. The daylight. He must milk the goats.

THAT evening, the crowd at The Liquid Loaf was like nothing Arthur had experienced in all his years of hospitality. Word had spread that something special inhabited his cellar, and the curious had arrived from as far away as the city. Arthur, who had spent a restorative afternoon weeding the kitchen gardens, taking money from the old ladies with their digestive problems, and chasing those two hungry blond kids away from the hole they'd chewed in his fence, wasn't expecting the onslaught. He'd nearly convinced himself that his reaction to the sculpture that morning had been the residue of a nasty dream.

The mass of grinning, titillated bankers from the city pressing themselves against the stone door of his cellar persuaded him otherwise. Nonetheless, recognizing an opportunity to market his craft beer that wouldn't come a second time, he welcomed the newcomers and opened a half hour early. Pleased by the success of his enterprise.

Until a fight broke out over who would sit nearest the sculpture. Until a wooden stool was broken. And until, wandering among them, selling his beer and his way of life, from packed table to packed table, he heard their muttered, snickering remarks about his sculpture. He was ashamed to look in its direction.

"Dear God, it *is* her. That one. You know—"

"Look at the expression on its face. So angry. But, you know, at the same time—"

"Do its clothes come off, do you think? The coat—"

"The coat, maybe. But not the shoes. Never the shoes."

"I myself am partial to the hat. Cozy." Gesturing for a third pint.

"Agreed, then. Leave the fuzzy hat and the shoes. The rest—"

Arthur smashed a bottle of beer against the bar. And then another. And another. In the stunned silence that followed, he glowered at the room with bloodshot eyes, his beard standing on end. "What is *wrong* with you people? You're sick. Out! All of you."

"Now, wait a minute. We've paid for—"

"Out! And if I ever see you here again, I'll get my rifle."

"Rifle?" Giggling. "Jesus, this really is the untouched wilderness. Who knows? Maybe that's his sister up there—"

The cellar emptied. And Arthur sat hunched in the chair before the dais, his fists pressed into his eyes. It wasn't yet ten in the evening.

But a moment or two later, he felt Hannah rest her hand on his shoulder. Pull a second chair across the sticky flagstone floor to sit beside him. "I've changed my mind again," she said after a quiet minute. "Get rid of it. It's bad luck."

He shook his head, his fists still crammed to his face.

"If you feel uncomfortable moving it," she said, "I'll do it for you. I'll take it to the dump. We'll recover the expense in less than a month."

He dropped his hands to his lap and blinked into the dim expanse of the cellar. Bursts of bright black light behind his eyes. A few empty glasses, haloed, scattered over damp tables. "Do you think she's cold?" His voice was dull. "She hasn't got enough clothing. She needs more."

"What?"

"The girl. I think she's cold."

"Arthur." Delicately evenhanded. "It isn't a girl. It's an object."

"She's shivering."

Hannah wrapped her arms around her waist. Cold herself now. "It's a bit of mangy 'art' that you purchased from a stinking pedophile who thought it would be fun to commemorate a notorious child rape."

"She's also frightened. Though she won't show it. Too proud."

Hannah worked to keep her voice reasonable. "I understand why it's affecting you, Arthur. It's disturbing. And I grant he's done a decent job with it. It's just different enough from the original to make it acceptable. Sufficiently grotesque and unreal that people can stare at it and sneer at it without—without shame. But if you look at it carefully, you can see that it's her. Poor girl. It's horrifying."

"Her little hands are so cold," he continued as though she hadn't spoken. "They're blue with cold. Tiny and blue."

And then, having always found neurosis boring, having chosen Arthur precisely for his stability and his good humor, Hannah exploded. Shot to her feet. "The thing was always blue, Arthur! You *bought* it blue. In the shop. Blue and wrinkly and weird. Next you'll be saying it's hungry!"

When he didn't reply, she drew an angry breath. "I love you because you're sane, Arthur. Because you take pleasure in—in curing meat and gathering calendula and fleecing bitchy old women. I need you like that. Not like this. I don't even recognize you now." She drew another breath and waited for a response. When none came, she continued, quiet now: "either that's gone or I'm gone. Tomorrow."

She waited. He said nothing. She climbed the stairs.

Having scarcely noticed her departure, Arthur took the sculpture's small hands in his own. He could encircle its wrists with a thumb and index finger. Which he did. For the feel of it. He'd been correct about the chill. The child was frozen.

Then, a thought occurred to him. Not all the old women were bitchy. Dropping the girl-thing's hands, he rushed upstairs to the restaurant. Rummaged about in the register. Retrieved what he wanted and jogged back to the cellar. Nearly falling to his knees along the way.

Two gossamer thin, unusually warm, red silk gloves. Wrinkling his forehead, not daring to breathe, he slid the gloves over the sculpture's fingers. Straightening each invisible seam with immeasurable care. After that, he stepped back and considered the result. It looked warmer. Tormented and angry still—a hint of humiliation— but warmer.

He noticed another beetle dropping to the sculpture's face. Quickly, before it reached her lips, he scooped it up and crushed it against the wall. He'd care for the girl. She no longer had any need to worry.

Moss

THEY'D clear-cut the small plot of forest across from Charon's house on the twelfth of February, three years before. Less than a month after his wife's fall. A not entirely accidental fall— his wife preferring a quick, crushed parietal to the vascular dementia she'd said she could feel and, worse, hear scraping its creeping way across her spongy brain. Charon had tried not to blame his wife. She'd been thinking of him, of his life, as well. Pride. But also compassion.

He certainly refused to fault the logging company. Doing so would have linked, in his own porous mind, that portly timber magnate, the one with the children—with the taste for children— forever to Charon's valiant, brilliant wife. It was a link he knew he'd never sunder once he'd forged it. And so, he didn't consider it. Less intelligent than his wife, perhaps, but always firmer. He'd have fought the thing in the brain indefinitely. No surrender.

More than that, though, Charon and his wife had always known, since they'd moved into the tiny A-frame house in the woods, that it was properly "in the woods" only on three sides. The fourth side, to the east, across the road, belonged to the Company. Forever vulnerable to the chop. Surprising it had lasted as long as it had.

The machines had worked for only two weeks felling the cedars. It was, after all, a small plot of land. And during that time, Charon had remained in the house, facing north, observing the sword ferns pushing up their early growth. Tiny, ephemeral fronds rising from ancient, Cretaceous rhizomes. Mocking the frenetic activity on the other side of the road. He also drank a great deal of mushroom tea.

When the trucks had departed, Charon had left his stained and empty teacup on the windowsill and had forced himself to examine the front of his house. The east side. It was nine in the morning, though he didn't know the day or, with certainty, the month. He opened the door for the first time in two weeks. Gagged on a swell of mucus in his contracted throat.

Across from him was a caricature of a battleground. A stage set of a modernist performance of the First World War. A bit of mist. Though less than he and his wife were accustomed to seeing on a March—he decided, arbitrarily, that it was March—morning. And beneath that, grey mud, grey stumps, wrecks of grey trunks leaning drunkenly against mounded gravel. Five or six thin, stunted alder trees scattered, still living, across the devastation. And one young cedar, chaotically spared, its lower branches gone, but otherwise untouched.

Charon closed the door. Stared at the door. Felt violated. And then, with an effort, he pushed that reaction, the wrong reaction, into his stomach, where it festered but no longer demanded his attention. As his wife would have reminded him before her brain's blood vessels had taken on a life of their own, empathizing with the forest was, at best, narcissistic. The trees didn't need his rape narrative.

He wouldn't blame the logging company. He wouldn't let its florid, gluttonous owner occupy his mind. He wouldn't connect the blotted, ugly thing across the road to his wife's wounded brain or to her body's doll-like fall. He blinked. He wasn't certain what he would do instead. But not that.

A moment or two later, he noticed the window to the side of the door. For the first time since they'd inhabited the house, a dawn sunbeam shone through it. Strong, white light slicing the knotted pine floor into precise squares of dark and bright. Bits of dust floating, nearly immobile, outside of time, in the shaft. Feeling a residual hint of the mushroom tea trickle across his sensory cortex, he shoved an experimental hand into the light. Twisted it backward and forward. The play of shadows over protruding, blue veins. Warm. He didn't know how he felt about warm.

But an idea struck him, in the sunbeam, before he descended into renewed tea and indolence. He would go back outside. He would appropriate the light in the way that the Company had appropriated the trees.

And so, avoiding the view across the road, he turned his back on the blight and contemplated the front of his house. It was suffused with sunshine. Almost hot. Early spring had brought the moisture that blanketed the property—the dew, the mist, what may have been rain, always rain—into blinding, white relief. Charon retrieved a childhood memory, long since scarred over, of a cool garden, in sunlight.

Confused, he pressed his lips together and returned to the dim interior of the house. His wife had scoffed at flower gardens. No plant, he could hear her saying, that either of them might bring to the property could match what was already there. The moss, the ferns, the lichen, the thousand-year-old trees unrivaled anywhere in the world. Why introduce some disease-ridden hybrid tea rose into the mix?

And indeed, in the early days, when Charon would sheepishly plant a few narcissus bulbs or a hydrangea start, the plants would endure, anemic, for a year, or perhaps three, before disappearing under the onslaught of the exuberant native growth. He frowned at the sunbeam. It had gathered strength. And moved. It looked alive and young.

He turned away from it and crept back to his chair on the north side of the house. Looked out at the ferns. Lifted his cup of mushroom tea, realized it was long since empty, and set it back on the table. Then he came to a decision. Next month was April. A good month to buy a flower. One that enjoyed morning light.

CHARON hadn't purchased a plant for twenty-five years, and when he'd last visited a garden center, the space had been attached to the local grocer's. His chosen nursery's painstakingly curated grounds and boisterous insistence on aspirational life choices—meditative, cottage, or Mediterranean, geisha, hedge witch, or Borgia— thus left him perturbed. This was the less intimidating nursery. He'd been frightened even to approach the ones advertising Andean tubers and mason bees.

But Charon was also old—confident in his experience—and he was unwilling to buckle in the face of the healthy, inhuman children staffing the business. As he wandered, sniffing dianthus and running his fingertips over lacey delphinium foliage, he began to enjoy the show. A carnival. Brightly lacquered shells of people, spinning past him, impervious to the decay that had taken his wife. He liked the smell of the place too. Not wild. Not forest-musky. Cultivated. Meant for light, lifestyle-conscious consumption.

ON THE NATURE OF THINGS

After an hour of hazy searching, vague smiles at customers nearly as old as he was and workers younger than his grandchildren, Charon stopped at a table on the far end of the "perennials" section. Only half-complete. A girl was preparing the display. Behind her, he could see wide, flared flowers in pink, yellow, and coffee-brown. Flowers as big as his spread hand. White stamens dripping orange pollen. Striped and speckled. Grotesque.

Lilies, he told himself. He hadn't noticed lilies since his childhood. Something about his mother's anger at the pollen staining his clothing. But surely the lilies on the table were too early? He hesitated to ask what might be a stupid question.

"Forced," the girl said, reading his mind. "But lovely, don't you think?"

"Forced," he echoed. Uncomfortable. Then, gathering his wits: "do they like morning sunshine?"

"Cool sun. Keep their roots in the shade, and they'll be fine. Moss works as a mulch."

"Moss."

He wanted the pink one. He took it.

Then he threaded his way back to the sales register, pausing briefly to pick up a small, mass-produced resin owl that caught his eye. As he waited for the customers in front of him, purchasing compost and slug bait, he inhaled the sickly sweet odor of the plant. He adored it.

"Join our loyalty program?"

He forced his attention away from the lily. "I'm sorry?"

"If you'll let me take your name and address, I can add you to our loyalty program. You'll save money the next time you visit."

"Oh," he said. "Yes, of course."

He gave her the information she wanted. Certain he'd be returning very soon.

"'Karen,' you said?" She was wrinkling her forehead at him.

"No. Charon." He paused. "Like the ferryman."

"Oh." Recognition. "I see. I don't take the ferry. Don't have to because I live on this side. It must be an interesting job, though. Are you retired?"

He wrinkled his forehead in turn. And then: "Yes. Yes, I've retired."

"Well, enjoy your lily. Lovely plant."

She was already smiling at the next customer. Busy day.

He did not, after all, go back to the nursery that spring, though his lily flourished, despite having been forced. Once he was home, he'd found himself feeling ashamed of his impulse. And he began to shy away from an immediate return to the colorful, superficial grounds of the shop. His wife would have called the pink flower clownish. Contemptible.

She had liked moss. And she'd liked it with both intelligence and unflinching intensity. On the east side of the house, where the sun rose, she'd identified thirteen separate species of moss, which she would coax into growth with a spray bottle during the rare summer dry spells that afflicted their forest.

After that, her task complete, she would remind him that the genome of *Leucolepis acanthoneura*, or umbrella moss, was twice as long as that of the honey bee. Moss, she had said to him on protracted shadowy evenings, over a glass or two of wine, had existed for millions of years before plants with flowers and the animals that pollinated them. It had survived environments that would have demolished weaker organisms. Its genome proved it.

One night, feeling contentious, Charon had pointed out to her an article in the journal of the defunct geographical society that he had once patronized. "On the Genetics of Garden Ornamentals." The genome of the crown imperial fritillary, with its thick stalk, madcap orange flowers, and ostentatious, eccentric leaves was forty times longer than that of the human genome. Five hundred times longer than the honey bee's. One of the longest ever studied. Surely, he'd said, aggressively meek, bryophytes had more to recommend them than a modestly complex set of DNA base pairs.

His wife had sneered. The imperial fritillary, she had retorted, was overbred, an appendage to human vanity. Whatever had elongated its genetic material was circular and repetitive, a dead end. Moss had come by its DNA honestly. It had survived. And, he had ventured, had humans also—survived? She hadn't deigned to answer.

Charon dismissed the memory as he left the potted lily on the doorstep to examine the moss, a transparent glass-green carpet, pulpy in the morning sun. Critical. He didn't believe that the brief hours of light that now shone on it would damage it. If anything, it appeared to be stretching. Unfolding. Luxuriating in the change. Snake liverwort with its reptilian scales, rough to the fingertip. Common smoothcap, throwing up its insectoid, reddish, needle-like capsule lids. Curly hypnum, densely matted, evoking sleep. Oblivion. Charon rubbed his nose with a knuckle.

To plant the lily, he would need to remove a small circle of moss and dig a proper hole. Fill it with potting soil and fertilizer. But he couldn't bring himself to choose which section of the moss to sacrifice. He couldn't make the first cut. Gripping the handle of the shovel he had found in the shed, he reprimanded himself. It was *not* a sacrifice. Not a cut. It was a move. He would move it. Gently. To the north side of the house, where it would be happier anyway.

Having brought himself out of his paralysis, he steeled his nerves and hacked through a soft mound of feather moss, *kindbergia praelonga*—his wife's least favorite—with the pointed end of the shovel. But the shovel stuck rather than cutting cleanly, the mat of dirt and moss clinging more than he'd expected it to. After three or four minutes of tugging, he left the shovel embedded in the hummock and went down on his hands and knees to pry at the green with his fingernails.

Eventually, he detached the feather moss from the ground and heaved it up against his chest. Shook a few earthworms back into the hole—they'd be useful to the lily. Felt a tight curl of nausea in his stomach as he saw that he'd also sliced through a nesting bumble bee. Told himself that the lily would do the remaining bees good. And then he staggered around the corner to deposit the muddy lump of moss in the shade.

By the time he returned to the east side of the house, he'd forgotten the dead bumble bee, the exposed earthworms, and the clenched grip of moss on earth. And the sight of the lighthearted pink lily in its pot, waiting for him on the doorstep, left him almost giddy. He began to whistle as he prepared the hole.

When he'd finished, having pressed the palms of his hands deep and splayed into the soil surrounding the lily, he felt his confused rage evaporate for a few, clean seconds. For the first time since the machines had left the forest, he no longer felt violated. He was at peace.

But still, he didn't return to the nursery that spring. Instead, he watched the single plant he'd purchased as it flowered longer than was reasonable. As it grew taller than any first-year nursery start ought to. As the remaining moss on the east side of the house crept across the outraged dirt he'd upturned, mulching and protecting its roots.

Nor did he return in the summer. Still feeling the dregs of an unexamined shame. Indeed, it was only in the autumn, when the catalogues began to arrive—addressed to "Karen," the nursery having sold his information to online purveyors of botanical products—that Charon considered expanding his garden. The catalogues, which he read with a purist student's diligence, promised him heirloom, doubled, hybrid, unheard-of cultivars of lily. Lilies he'd never find in the nursery. Lilies even his mushroom tea couldn't suggest to him.

And all within reach, provided he tucked the bulbs into the soil before the fifteenth of November. A magical date. He ordered every one of them. Unable to stop himself. And then, satisfied, he huddled on the north side of his house, waiting out the winter.

THE ensuing April, when the meaty spears of his earlier lily plants began to break the soil, little of the moss remained in the eastern sun. As Charon had planted his bulbs the October and November before, he'd quickly lost his squeamishness about ripping up the mats of translucent green. About disturbing, and sometimes dismembering, the sleeping bees. Most of the moss was now piled in a heap beyond the edge of the cedar forest, on the west side of the property. He assumed it was still alive. Bryophytes were survivors.

Lilies, contrarily, demanded care. He found himself patrolling the bed on warm mornings, inspecting the growth of the stalks, two, three, five times an hour. Crushing slugs between thumbnail and index finger. Anxiously inspecting smooth, unfolding leaves. Leaves so unlike moss. So unlike ferns or lichen. Silently reciting their musical names to himself. Their pedigrees.

For though he did appreciate the heirlooms—Formosa (1918), Black Beauty (1957—hardly an antique in his view, but such it was listed), Regale (1905), and Candidum (its origin Mesopotamian, Roman, something historic beyond imagination)—and though he enjoyed the demure species forms—drooping Amoenum, speckled Auratum, puckered Catesbaei, and black Eupetes, like something pressed against the window on a dark, hellish night—he preferred, above all, the hybrids. The plants bred large and fragrant for his pleasure. New varieties every year, built, *constructed*, for him.

Kamura Pyrotechnics with its splotch of dark red against a rangy white background. "Showy," said the catalogue. Sorrel Punch, blinding crimson, spiritual inheritor of a Jamaican rum drink he'd never known existed. Couldn't imagine. Peaches on Chocolate. Yellow, pink, brown, dotted—why did the hybridizers encourage his fantasies of tasting the flowers? And his favorite, Betty Sturley.

Betty Sturley had huge white and yellow flowers. Raised, almost diseased, spots. Six-inch stamens, dripping pollen. "Heavily papillate tipped red," noted the catalogue. Betty Sturley, Charon imagined, his interior voice dry, would not have impressed his wife. He didn't care. Pacing the eastern side of his house, he waited, watched, wrapped his fingers around the thickening stalks. Anticipating the long, pod-like buds.

And in the summer, his vigilance was rewarded. The lily bed sparkled glorious in the dawn sunlight, its heavy fragrance permeating the darkest, most mildewed corners of the A-frame. Every bulb had emerged. Every plant had gorged itself on the bone meal he'd fed to it. He'd engendered something beyond nature. Dazzling and heroic.

As a result, one hot day, a few weeks after the larger lilies had begun to unfurl, an old Morris Mini slowed to a halt, parking on the other side of the road. Against the clear-cut forest. A Purple Heart Veteran's license plate hanging a bit askew on the back. A man with a limp emerging and crossing to the garden.

Charon, studiously failing to notice, was, as always, on his hands and knees. Clearing away the whorls of moss that regrouped and spread whenever he wasn't properly attentive. His lilies no longer needed moss for mulch. Moss was a nuisance. A place for slugs to hide. He pretended not to see the man. Hoping to be left alone to his labor.

But the man wasn't to be deterred. Hobbling to a stop and considering the orderly growth, he said, "they're beautiful."

Charon sighed and stood. Faced the man. "Thank you."

"How long have you been working on them?"

"A little over a year." He glanced fondly at his first pink lily, well over four feet tall now, sporting eight swollen stems. "I bought the first one in a pot. Last April."

"Impossible." The man's smile was a trifle manic for a wounded veteran. "These must be at least five years old. Ten years old. They're positively Brobdingnagian."

Charon smiled as well. He enjoyed a literary reference. And the thought of something puny cowering beneath his towering lilies piqued a mild thrill.

The man squinted across the road at the open ground, which had begun cautiously healing itself. The battlefield had been softened by a swath of alder saplings and a sea of yellow ragwort. "It must be the sun. Ideal morning light for lilies." He paused. "You aren't worried about the cankerwort there reseeding all over your land?"

Charon glanced at the clear-cut. Ordinarily he managed not to notice it. He certainly hadn't considered the ragwort. His throat clenched as it hadn't for months. Then, willing himself to relax, he responded to the first part of the man's question. "Yes, I imagine it is the sunlight. They get four and a half hours this time of the year. Not too much, not too little."

"Well, it's that and your green thumb." The man's smile hadn't wavered.

Stupidly, Charon looked at his thumb.

"I'll be leaving you to it." The man began to turn. Then, as though remembering something, he pulled a small, pink card from his pocket. "There's a flower show at the botanical garden next Saturday. That couple—you know, with the gemstones and rare metals money—bought it, the botanical garden, that is, and they're wanting to show their public spirit. Winner gets a pair of scarce Cypripedium as first prize. You ought to bring Betty Sturley there. Cracker of a lily—she stands a better chance than many."

"Cypripedium?" Charon had scarcely heard the remainder of the man's statement. The word echoed through his brain like a strain of mushroom tea. Like a memory once cherished, but crushed by experience.

"Hmm." The man nodded. "A Lady's Slipper Orchid. Red one. Rare as bird's milk. Grown from unique seed collected in Asia." He squinted at the light shifting over the lily bed again. "In fact, you might consider branching out into the Himalayan species. They'd enjoy it here."

The man turned and left.

THE prize-giving for the flower show was held at the house of its patrons rather than at the botanical garden itself because one of them—the wife, Holly? Rose?—couldn't or wouldn't leave her bedroom. Eccentric, people said. Overly industrious. A creative type. But Charon, whose Betty Sturley had triumphed with grim inevitability over her competitors, found himself unable to appreciate the exquisite grounds of the property or its immense, and indeed Brobdingnagian, offering of saccharine edibles.

When the man had limped back to his clattering Morris Mini the previous week, Charon's health had begun—not to fail—but to metamorphose. Clutching the pink card, more pleased by the man's praise of his lilies than he had wanted to admit to himself, Charon had ventured inside, made himself a cup of weak chamomile tea, and settled into the chair overlooking the north part of his land. To think about entering the competition.

The sword ferns, he barely registered, were huge and healthy this time of year. The chunks of moss, piled haphazard on the west side of the house, were making inroads in their direction as well. And so, rather than dwelling on his successes, Charon began to fear that he was running out of room. Where might he put his lilies next year? His Himalayan species? His Cypripedium? Savoring the word. He frowned at the view. If he got rid of that old maple, there might just be sufficient light to—

A tingling ache in his right hand, like something icy shooting through his capillaries, interrupted the thought. He brought his hand into the cool, north light. Peered at his thumb. Something was wrong with it. A greenish, hair-like smudge had spread across the pad, obscuring the ridges.

Dirt from the lily bed, he told himself, wiping it on the arm of the chair. He examined it again. The green hadn't budged. In fact, squinting at it, he saw that it was spreading just beneath the top layer of his skin. It hadn't come from outside. Encircling his swollen knuckle it rippled under his epidermis, moving down toward his palm. Where it stopped. Inert.

He dropped his hand to the arm of his chair and half smiled. Glanced at his teacup. Chamomile, yes, but he'd never been fastidious about washing the dishes. This was the residual effect of something fungal that had stuck to the ceramic and found its devious way into his brain. The state of his hand was not, for Charon, an unfamiliar sensory experience. He simply hadn't solicited it this time.

Shaking his head, firm, he found a lily catalogue to peruse. Wasted the remainder of the day fantasizing about what he'd plant come autumn. And then, having heated a can of soup and washed his bowl and cup more vigorously than usual, he took himself off to his wide, and still lonely, bed.

The next morning, the green had spread to his wrist and lower arm. In addition to making use of his capillaries, the stuff was also producing a bristly green fuzz in place of the hairs on his skin.

ON THE NATURE OF THINGS

When he rubbed it off, it simply returned with more vigor. Becoming lumpy. A carpet. He'd had no tea for hours—couldn't blame the mushrooms this time—and so he decided to visit his wife's doctor. A practical woman, close to his own age, whom he'd avoided since medicine had fallen short in treating his wife's underlying condition: pride.

The doctor cleared her appointments to see him straight away. Guilt, he supposed, for failing to predict the crushed parietal. Good. He'd use that.

But when he revealed his ailment—complaint—change—he didn't know what to call it—the doctor's reaction wasn't what he'd hoped. The green had spread further. Producing a marbled effect over his shoulder and a not unpleasant pressure on the gland in the pit of his arm. But the doctor, though perplexed, was not unduly worried.

"This won't satisfy you," she eventually said, having gazed at it and prodded it with a gloved finger, "but I believe it's psychosomatic."

"Thanks." He was buttoning his shirt. "You're saying I've done it to myself?"

"No." Doubtful. "Not entirely. But look at it."

"Difficult not to, the way it's spreading."

She leaned back in her ergonomic chair and settled an ostentatiously traditional magnifying glass beside her on the desk. "I remember your wife telling me she grew moss. As a sort of hobby. Or study."

71

"Yes?"

"It's moss." She tapped a fingertip on the magnifying glass.

"It's not moss," he said. "I can feel it creeping about under my skin. Clogging my capillaries."

"Are you feeling discomfort?" Banal and professional.

"No."

"Difficulty breathing? Sleeping? Dizzy spells?"

"No."

"Do you dislike it?"

He thought in silence for more than a minute before responding. Cast the doctor a suspicious look. "No. No, I don't dislike it."

"Good. Does it help in alleviating your guilt?"

"*What?*"

"You survived."

He stood. "I'm leaving."

She stood too. "Very well. If you find that it becomes pathological—that is, if it interferes with your daily functioning or if it begins to cause you pain—please see me again. I'm always here for you, Charon."

He left without thanking her. Dissatisfied. Guilt was the least of his problems.

Yet now, accepting his award under the bright sunshine, his coveted pair of Cypripedioideae, from Clive—Clive, harassed and bilious, despite his menacing financial empire—

Charon was doubtful. The rhizoid tendrils of sometimes fuzzy, sometimes crystalline, brown, red, and olive had spread across most of his body over the past week. Always a millimeter beneath the surface of his skin. Curling and clumping. Bottle-glass ripples. While the hairs on his arms, chest, legs, and groin had turned a uniform silken, sporangia green.

And though, from a short distance, he looked merely like he spent a great deal of time in the garden, unable to dislodge the earth from his skin, nails, and hair, he knew that the transformation was deeper than that. Self-inflicted or not. He wondered whether, in fact, it *was* some visceral manifestation of guilt. A lingering shame. Staining and infiltrating his capillaries and keratinocytes.

As he gazed at the potted red slipper orchids he held in each hand, frowning at the polite applause of the botanical society members, he dismissed the thought. He was immune to guilt. Above shame. These intricately wrought flowers—unique outside the highest mountaintops of Bhutan—were all that he'd hoped for. The envy of any who beheld them. And vibrant, strong Betty Sturley, likewise immune to uncertainty, had conquered them for him. Guilt was an absurdity.

He swallowed a surge of pure pride at the sight of the plants. At the pleated, dark green leaves—the vertiginous, impossible fans, from which fragile, eighteen-inch stalks already bore red slippers the size of herons' eggs, each topped by three maroon petals, streaked with splatters of pus-colored flecks. The blossoms were like exquisite acts of violence. Formed as though whatever dainty, celestial Aphroditic foot had once worn the slipper had been sliced, whole, from its clumsy and tainted terrestrial body.

Charon shivered as he clutched the pots and pushed his way to his car, shaking off congratulatory remarks. Forced himself to smile, wan and quick, up at the pillowy face of Holly or Rose pressed against the highest window of the mansion's tower. Spreading, fleshy and massive, across the entirety of the glass, looking down at the celebration she'd engendered. Eating something sticky and pink. Directing a futile and malignant scrutiny toward the silent, needle-like woman knitting something complex in a chair on the turf at the far end of the catering tables.

He also scarcely noticed when the pretty blonde girl sank her teeth into his ankle. Though it did slow his pace until the robust, equally blond, boy pulled her off. Apologizing.

"Forgive us, sir. My sister has made a mistake."

The girl turned on him. "It wasn't a mistake. Spikemoss. I smelled it. I *tasted* it. It's inside him. He's got it all over, in his—"

"*Not now.*" The boy raised his face, clean and polite, to Charon's. "Congratulations, sir. They're beautiful flowers. Like tiny, bleeding shoes."

ON THE NATURE OF THINGS

Charon blinked down at his plants. Returned his attention to the children, about to say something to the nice, well-brought-up boy. But the boy was already gone, dragging his sister along with him. Toward that splintered mess at the end of the drive that may once have been a carving of a duck. Or perhaps some sort of basket.

It didn't matter. He had more important things to do. He wanted the plants in the ground, on the northeast side of his house, now. Right now. He'd compost the moss he'd piled there. His Himalayan garden would begin tonight.

OVER the next months, Charon's rare Cypripedium, having replaced the moss, throve and multiplied, just as his lilies had. And once he'd cut down the maple tree, he had space and light to experiment with giant Himalayan, and delicate, bell-like Mackliniae, species. They all sprouted or spread monstrously, colonizing and pushing back both the ferns and the now nearly non-existent moss.

Better still, he no longer noticed his lumped, spongy skin or his green, glass-like body hair. Taking pleasure, instead, in the increasing pressure on his glands, under his arms, in his neck, at the intersection of leg and torso—not to mention the fluttering of microscopic spores coursing throughout his veins and arteries. Rarely leaving the house, he encountered no one who might comment on his changed appearance. His bulbs and seeds he ordered from catalogues. His mushrooms he gathered in the forest. And he had sufficient cans of soup to last a lifetime.

Until one summer morning, the Morris Mini returned to the side of the road nearest the clear-cut, and the limping soldier emerged. As he clattered across to the lily bed on the east side of the house, Charon strode out to meet him, hating himself for his eagerness to display his flowers. The man greeted Charon, politely failing to notice the state of his skin and hair. And then he spied the plot of Cypripedium, like a spot of bloody viscera, and allowed Charon to lead him to it.

"So, Betty Sturley did you proud," he said. "I thought she might."

"I also took your advice on the giant Himalayan lilies," Charon replied. Shy.

The man gazed up at them. A grove. Already flowering. "Astonishing. They must be fifteen feet high. I've never seen their like outside of China."

"You've seen them beyond cultivation?"

"Hmm." The man scratched his cheek. "I helped describe and name them. For European taxonomy, that is. Nothing new to the natives, of course. Cardiocrinum."

Charon felt a murmuring strand of something green caress and then wrap itself around an artery deep inside his chest. But he was familiar by now with the use that the tendrils made of his body. More perplexing to him was the man's claim. He blinked. "But surely the giant lily was identified in the 1820s. Nathaniel Wallich's work for the East India Company." He stopped short, not wanting to sound pedantic. "I've been reading catalogues."

"I can see that you have." The man was still admiring the towering lilies. "Capital work. Cardiocrinum," he repeated. "Heart Lily."

Charon felt short of breath. "From the shape of the leaves."

"If you say so." The man turned his attention to the red Cypripedium. "And these are simply wild about you, aren't they? Couldn't have found a better home."

Charon, his chest now constricting under what felt like a thousand spongy strands piercing and filling his aorta and lungs, nodded. He couldn't reply.

The man squatted beside one of the red lady's slippers, his limp apparently gone. He pushed a thick index finger into the pouch and extracted a few drops of liquid. "You see. This is how they reproduce. Trap the pollinator in the fluid, keep it immobile for a day or two, and then allow it to go free covered in pollen. Try it."

Charon fell to his knees and found himself, not knowing how, with each of his fingers immersed, clenched, in one of the bloody red pouches. He couldn't extract them. He couldn't move his legs. He couldn't breathe. The green had colonized his heart and lungs. And, worse, he could feel it, *hear* it, scraping away at the lower part of his brain. Moving outward and upward. Toward

his frontal lobe. A film of reddish green descending over his eyes.

The man dusted off his knees and stood. "I'll leave you to it, then." As he returned to his car, he twisted back. "I didn't want to tell you before, but I noticed kudzu growing among the alders and cankerwort in that lot across the street. Terrible nuisance, kudzu. Once it gets hold of a property, you might as well give up and move." He chuckled to himself. "*Move.*"

Charon tensed, to the extent that he was able, at the thought of kudzu, not to mention ragwort and alder, making inroads into his lily beds. But then, recalled to his immediate situation, he rallied what remained of his mind. The bits not given over to spikemoss and smoothcap, liverwort and hypnum. He would fight this. Unlike his wife, he would not let it defeat him. He would reclaim his epidermis and his aorta, his follicles and his keratin. He wouldn't let them go.

Besides, bryophytes were primitive. Undeveloped. No match for the complexity of an organism such as himself. His only real concern was who would care for the lilies as he recovered. In the meantime.

FUR

VIVIAN left Arthur when she lost her job at the bank. The behemoth hedge fund had swallowed up her section, leaving her two senior colleagues with something of an inheritance, but she herself blindsided and unprepared, with nothing. Nothing, that is, aside from the cat—though she didn't want to begin there. The cat was an afterthought.

She hadn't told Arthur her reasons for leaving him. Unable to find words to explain that she'd adored him as an expensive and esoteric hobby, had delighted in subsidizing his goats, his bees, his sausages, and his beer, but that she couldn't keep him without the ongoing and not insignificant support of the bank. He'd have been wounded. Believing himself solvent—a savvy and responsible businessman and professional. She couldn't do that to him.

And so, she'd disappeared on a glacial winter night, leaving neither note nor forwarding address. She'd also taken the cat. The lynx. The tawny, tufted Canada lynx, built like a shy, furry Muppet, with its high hind legs and ungainly paws, that had found the outside of their glass door a congenial spot to spend the rare snowy, and less rare frosty, winter night. They'd called it "Thor."

She hadn't, it's true, meant to abscond with the lynx. It had simply appeared the evening after her desertion, pressed against the window of her own, far less pastoral, "village" townhouse. She'd been staring at her savings account, concluding with a tight twist of anxiety that she could continue for perhaps five further months before she'd default on her mortgage. When she'd looked up from the screen, and there was Thor. A broad, coarse face, cartoonishly demonic, stretched out against the black glass slider.

She'd also not meant to let the cat indoors. They'd certainly never done so when it had turned up in Arthur's meadow. Tailless, a good four feet tall at the shoulder, and wearing an implacable predator's expression, the antithesis of domestic, it was not an animal to take as a pet. But Vivian hadn't been feeling rational or interested in exotic animal best practices when it had turned up at her door. If it mauled her, it would take her mind off her financial worries. If it didn't, well, having it in the house would also take her mind off her financial worries.

She had opened the door. And Thor, the lynx, had behaved neither like a domestic cat nor like a wild animal. Without hesitation, without betraying the slightest hint of fear of the unfamiliar, suburban environment, it had entered. Looking neither right nor left—neither at the coat closet with the white, plastic shutters nor at the breakfast nook with the brown plastic flooring—it had padded across the synthetic Berber carpet to Vivian's living room.

The quartzite slab in the open-concept kitchen failed to impress it. It was unmoved by the propane and ceramic fireplace, ignited via a button near the window overlooking the patio. But Vivian's leather recliner with the vibration and heat massage options had given it pause. It had halted in front of the elongated foot rest. Turned its thick neck in Vivian's direction. Examined the chair again.

With an inward shrug, Vivian had approached the chair, skirted the lynx, which held its position, giving her little room to position herself, and relaxed into the recliner. Once she was settled, Thor leapt into her lap, landing with sufficient force to wind her for three or four seconds. Leaving her arms briefly paralyzed.

Soon, though, when she was breathing normally again, the cat was kneading her stomach with paws the size of her own hands, its black claws only partially retracted. Ripping rents in the grubby t-shirt she wore to sleep. A low rumble in the back of its throat. Its prickly head pressed against her sternum, the feather-like tufts of black on its ears tickling the sides of her neck. A touch of drool. Thor was an insistent and needy cat. She patted its roiling back with the palm of her hand a feeble two or three times.

Unwilling to risk pushing the cat off her stomach, Vivian had shifted herself into a more comfortable position on the recliner. Hoping that it would bore itself and jump off on its own to explore the remainder of what she admitted was a less than compelling townhouse. Before she could begin to worry, however, she herself had fallen asleep. The anxiety of her existential situation transmuting into exhaustion and welcome unconsciousness. When she'd woken the next morning, Thor was gone. It had never occurred to her to feed it.

THE lynx returned the next evening, and Vivian let it into the house. Allowed it to burrow into her chest and belly, salivating and grunting as it pushed against her flesh. Still, she didn't think to feed it. It left by morning.

On the third night, she was expecting it. But when it crept through the narrow hall into her living room, she could see that something was wrong. It limped, propelling itself via short, ungainly hops, and the rumble it emitted from its throat was periodically broken by a high, kitten-like mew. It smelled of the arctic punctuated by fear.

It was also unwilling to jump onto the recliner, preferring to curl up in front of the propane fire, obscuring the hand-tufted hearth rug from the ethical home design store in the city. Vivian knelt beside it, rubbing its dense fur with outstretched fingers. Fell asleep with her cheek against its coarse hind leg.

The next morning, Thor was still lying by the fire. Its eyes were dim, and a fever trickled through its fur. Its paws were swollen even beyond their ordinary comic width. Vivian brought it a saucer of milk—uncertain what else to offer—but it scarcely noticed. Its breath was labored.

Pulling a new t-shirt over her yoga bottoms, she decided to take it to a vet. Maneuver it to a vet. A challenging task that involved, first, coaxing it out of the house, down the stairs, and into the collective garage she shared with the other owners in the townhouse community.

She had no fear of the disapproval of intrusive neighbors. They were an affluent and affable lot, above aspirational, lace-curtain adherence to by-laws or house rules. But the lynx itself was groggy. Unable to move with its effective, if clumsy, stealth. And Vivian felt self-conscious dragging an exotic cat through her community's suburban landscaping. Past the clumps of daylilies. Over the fescue.

Nonetheless, by the time she and Thor had reached her four-cylinder BMW—she'd be breaking her lease and returning it sometime in the next week—they'd developed something of a rhythm. And the lynx heaved itself into the rear seats of the car without Vivian doing more than opening the door and pointing. It then stretched on its side, its eyes closed, throughout the thirty-minute drive to the only vet Vivian knew in the area. A horse specialist. But he had a lucrative side-business in lap dogs bred for respiratory problems and aristocratic kittens with nubs of vestigial ears. Complex animals. She imagined he could cope with a lynx's injured paw.

She wasn't disappointed. The vet kept them waiting for less than an hour and then put Thor under with a quick, practiced flick of ketamine in order to examine its feet. He took his time, intrigued. And when he'd finished, he led Vivian out to the corridor to discuss the situation.

"Its footpads are lacerated beyond anything I've ever seen." He was removing thin, blue surgical gloves. "I'm surprised it could even move from your car to the building."

"Oh." She felt a pang of guilt about the fescue.

"It looks as though it's been walking over hot coal and glass. For hundreds of miles. Have you any idea where it could have encountered that sort of environment?"

She shook her head. And then: "can you heal it? Is there a—a procedure of some sort?"

"It's expensive."

She smiled. Of course. "I understand."

She'd return the BMW this afternoon. Default on her other loans a few months early.

Better than grimly waiting out the inevitable. Thor had done her a favor.

"I can reconstruct them." The vet interrupted her brooding. "The process is similar to what we do with human burn victims. It ought to take six surgeries. Five weeks total. We'll keep the cat here for observation throughout."

Five weeks. She nodded slowly. If she didn't eat, she'd still have a month or two in her townhouse along with something left over to cover the bill. "Okay."

He nodded, curt and businesslike. An attitude to calm panicking pet owners. "Excellent. If you'll leave your information with Anita at the front desk, we'll contact you when—" he frowned. "I'm sorry, what was the cat's name?"

"It's a lynx."

"Yes." He looked about to smile. "I'm a vet."

"Sorry."

"Its name?"

"Thor."

"Good. We'll contact you when Thor is up and about again."

She turned, feeling bullied by both vet and lynx—tangible memory of the latter's fist-like paws kneading her stomach—but before she pushed through the swinging door to find Anita, the vet stopped her again. "It's a magnificent animal. Where did you find it?"

She blinked. "It followed me home."

"Lucky you." He disappeared into the consulting room.

And Vivian left her name and address with the receptionist.

PRECISELY five weeks later, wearing the same t-shirt and yoga bottoms, digging instant noodles out of a Styrofoam container in her breakfast nook, Vivian received news from the vet's office. Thor was healthy and recovered. She could retrieve the cat at her convenience. They'd send the bill in the mail.

She wasted no time. Jogging past the fescue and daylily, which had neither grown nor changed shape in the intervening weeks—she suspected they might also be made of plastic—she climbed into her pickup truck. Forty years old, rusted yellow paint, and purchased for three hundred dollars from a lot beyond the Institute, it also had a V-8 engine that made Vivian happier than her BMW's motor ever had. The gurgle sounded like the lynx's when it was forgetting to retract its black claws from her belly. Ripping holes in her sweater.

As she drove, though, she worried. Worried that Thor would have forgotten her. Worried that the bill would be more than she could afford. Chiding herself at the same time. The lynx was a wild animal. It didn't matter whether it remembered her. She'd be returning it to the forest. Far away in the forest. And even if she wanted to keep it, which was an absurdity, she had no room. Soon, she'd have no house. Which also left the problem of the vet's bill somewhat academic.

She was, nonetheless, pleased when Thor leapt from the examination table upon her appearance in the consulting room. Padded over to her, easily shrugging off the vet's restraining hand, and shoved its head into her stomach. Covering her sneakers with its rehabilitated paws.

Even more than pleased, though, Vivian was astonished. As Thor had pushed through the air, she'd seen the undersides of the cat's footpads. They were garish. Swaths of magenta, turquoise, and yellow. Smaller spots of pink and lime-green. She stared at the vet.

"Yes," he said. "I fear I neglected to mention it before. We use synthetic grafts to re-grow the skin. The colors are unpredictable. And the finished product doesn't take to dye."

The lynx was sitting back on its hind legs. Bathing a front paw. Its claws extended. Preening. Looking almost pleased with itself.

"Will they interfere with—with its ability to hunt?" She tried, experimentally, to pat Thor on the head. "Can it still feed itself? Hide from danger?" She felt ignorant. Uncertain of what she was asking. "That sort of thing?"

"Of course." The vet was losing interest again. "By the time prey sees the undersides of its paws, it's a bit too late for evasive action. Don't you think?"

"Yes. Yes, I suppose so." She removed her hand. "Thank you again for this—remarkable— work."

"The bill is in the mail."

She led Thor out to the waiting truck. And the lynx rode home in the passenger's seat. Disdaining, as she'd imagined it would, an exposed journey in the bed.

That evening, she slept in the recliner once again. Thor, flexing his natty, reconstructed footpads, spread itself across her lap. And was gone the next morning.

For a further two weeks, they kept to their routine. The lynx would press its face against her dark window, she would let it into the townhouse, and it would sprawl, rumbling, over her chest and stomach for the remainder of the night. Stifling, uncomfortable, and endearing.

Until, having spent a queasy morning viewing her dwindling savings account, Vivian had forced herself into action. She couldn't pretend that her situation was sustainable. That her nightly interludes with the cat would continue indefinitely. Or that they ought to. The lynx was a wild animal. It belonged in the wild.

And so, on a cold Saturday night, the smell of beer and pizza drifting from the windows of the other breakfast nooks—the scent of the employed enjoying their weekends—Vivian led Thor to her pickup truck. The cat followed willingly. Hopped into the passenger seat without demur. Remained docile as she drove the two hours to the dense forest waste beyond the Institute. It was an uncultivated region she ordinarily avoided, a place where people disappeared. Where things were lost.

She left the truck at the side of a ditch running along the wood's edge and cajoled Thor into the thin trees that curtained the darker core of the forest. Then, her fingertips on the cat's rough neck, she walked with it for twenty minutes until she could no longer see the stars through the canopy. Refusing to succumb to the temptation to bury her face in the lynx's fur, she stepped back and scratched her temple.

"Stay here, Thor." She felt an idiot speaking to it.

Thor remained motionless, sitting on its hind legs. Bored.

"Good."

She turned and found her way back to the road. Exhaled, relieved and embarrassed, when she saw her truck. She'd felt a soft breath of fear, for perhaps forty-five seconds, five minutes into her return walk, that she'd lost her way. Shivered. She had no intention of revisiting the wood. Not being wild herself.

VIVIAN'S situation declined after she left Thor in the forest, despite her anemic assumption the previous week that she'd reached the nadir of her fortunes. The mortgage company raised the interest rates on her townhouse, leaving her uncertain that she could manage even a full month before defaulting on the loan. The BMW dealership took her to small claims court over her broken lease. The driver's side window of her pickup truck jammed, leaving her frigid, and frequently damp, whenever she drove it, sparingly, conserving petrol, to the convenience store for food. And her yoga bottoms ripped in one knee. She sat on the floor, on the hand-tufted hearth rug, and cried after the last of these assaults on her dignity.

When, two weeks after losing the lynx, the bell of her townhouse door rang, she nearly didn't answer. Stretched on her recliner, eating dry noodles from a cup to which she hadn't troubled to add water. But after it rang a second time, insistent, she dropped the cup on the floor and rose from the chair. Chance callers would at least represent a break in the monotony. Perhaps they were selling something.

She pulled her hair into a pink elastic, checked to be certain that she was fully, if not hygienically, dressed, and walked to the front door. Pulled it open. Saw Thor. Sitting smug and fat beside a healthy, nicely groomed young man. Dark hair, clean shaven, smelling of prosperity. Symmetrical, non-threatening features. Clothing of quiet good taste. The sort of man she'd been pleased to avoid in favor of burdensome, labor-intensive people like Arthur when she'd been attached to the bank.

"Yes?" She refused to acknowledge the lynx. Couldn't cope with another lawsuit. God knows what the animal had done. The cat looked more than smug, she decided as it bathed a turquoise paw. Self-important.

"Forgive me," the man began, typically for his type. She was already irritated. "But this—uh—Thor belongs to you, if I'm not mistaken?"

She narrowed her eyes at him. "What do you mean, 'Thor?'"

He held up his phone. "My phone picked up the information from its tracking chip. In the shoulder, I think? This is you, isn't it?"

She examined the screen. Read through the detailed information she'd provided Anita. The vet must have inserted the chip under Thor's skin. Neglected to tell her. She ought to have read the bill more carefully. "Yes, it's mine. What's it done?"

"Killed my rabbits," the man said.

"So?" she began, on the defensive. "It's a cat. That's what cats do. You should know better than to—"

"Actually, I wanted to thank you for it." He sounded embarrassed to have spoken over her. Unused to conversational aggression. "They were a nuisance. Eating my roses. I'd tried everything to get rid of them before, um, Thor appeared."

"You grow roses?"

"Yes." He smiled his non-threatening smile. "May I come in?"

"No."

The man blinked. Surprised. And interested. A masochist, presumably. Which was a

scenario Vivian didn't have the energy to contemplate at the moment.

"Thanks for bringing back my cat." She opened the door wider. Thor padded inside. She shut the door in the man's face.

"My name is Talius," he said as the door closed.

When the lynx was inside, Vivian smiled at it, despite herself. She didn't want to admit how pleased she was to see it again. But Thor was uninterested in her emotional reaction to its return. The cat pushed itself into the living room and sat, expectant, in front of her recliner. It was eleven in the morning. But what did that matter? Having nothing else to do, Vivian sat in the chair, allowed the lynx to spread itself on top of her, and slept throughout the afternoon and evening. By morning, Thor was gone.

The cat returned for three consecutive evenings, reestablishing with insulting confidence their earlier habits. On the fourth night, however, Vivian felt a pang of something like wounded pride, something like conscience, at her willingness to be led. This life, suspended, repetitive, and drowsy, couldn't continue. As much as she was enjoying it. As much as she was missing it with a drugged, melancholic ache even before she'd lost it.

And so, at midnight on the fifth night, she brought Thor to her truck, drove them back to the forest, and walked with the lynx further into the trees than she had before. Feeling the hostile animosity of the wood almost before she'd crossed its threshold. This time, she didn't tell the lynx to stay. Shivering, confused, and addled in the darkness, she simply turned and fled. Trusting Thor to play the wild animal's part. She must find a job.

But three days later, as she scoured the internet for demeaning entry-level finance positions, her phone rang. Pleased to be distracted from her pursuit, she answered without checking the screen.

"Forgive me for troubling you again." She stifled a sigh. "It's Talius."

"Yes?"

"I'm afraid that Thor has made a reappearance."

"Eating your rabbits?"

"Yes." A smile in the voice. "It also killed two deer. I hadn't realized that lynxes were capable of hunting large game. It *is* a lynx, correct?"

"Yes. I'm sorry about the deer."

"No worries. They're a nuisance too."

"Oh. Good." She had already returned her attention to the job ads. "Look, do you think you could bring it back here? I know it's asking a lot, but I'd be grateful—"

"Hmm." More apologetic than before, if that was possible. "You see, the difficulty is that Thor refuses to budge."

"Oh."

"You needn't concern yourself. It hasn't done any damage. But I can't seem to convince it to move beyond the end of my drive." He paused. "Would you be willing to try yourself? Enticing it back, that is."

"The end of your drive, you say?" At least he wasn't asking her to enter his home. She didn't trust the meekness.

"Yes. If you've got a pencil handy, I'll give you the address now."

"Fine." Better, at any rate, than reading employment websites. She copied the information. "I'll be there in forty-five minutes."

SHE didn't trouble to change out of her sweats before starting her gurgling, yellow truck and driving in search of Thor. Though the address that Talius had given her was at the center of an enclave of repressive, and massive, properties hidden behind gates and hedges that, unlike those of her townhouse or even of Arthur's meadow, served their defensive purpose. Because of that. She refused to be intimidated.

But when she reached the house, she realized that she needn't have worried either way about dressing to be received. "The end of the drive" was far enough from the entrance to the property—a building shrouded in a thick hedge of wickedly barbed roses so high that its uppermost canes were lost in a wet mist—that no one would see her as anything other than a blot on the horizon. A bit of landscape rather than a person.

Sitting prim and unassuming to the side of the drive, beneath the low arched entrance to a footpath, was Thor. And beside the cat stood Talius, wearing a dark, similarly unassuming sweater. Shoes that she sensed would have paid for six months of her mortgage.

"Forgive me," he said.

She pushed down a snide retort. Beginning to fear, neurotic, that he was in fact doing something that required forgiveness. Though she had no notion of what that activity might be.

"My fault," she replied. Short. "I can't think why it keeps turning up here."

"They like rabbits." Talius pushed his hands into his pockets.

All right. She didn't want to make conversation. "Thank you again. I'll get it into the truck—"

But before she could complete her sentence, the lynx, overjoyed to see her, bounded across the path, shoved its wide, clownish paws against her shoulders, neglected to retract its claws, and shredded her top. Her skin it left unmarked.

She was now standing half-naked, bare-chested, in front of Talius.

"Jesus." She covered herself with her arms.

"Oh dear." Talius held out a sympathetic hand. Thought better of it. Hugged his waist. Actually blushed. "I'm so very sorry."

"Why are *you* sorry?" She was glaring at Thor, frenetic and satisfied, padding between them. Brushing their legs. Like some eager-to-please dog. Disgraceful.

"Vivian," he said, addressing her by name for the first time. "You must come inside. I'll find you something to wear. This is ghastly. You can't leave like this."

She stared at his mild features. His embarrassment. Her distrust grew. "No. I'll be fine. I'll get Thor into the truck, and then—and then I'll drive home. It isn't far."

Notwithstanding her practical tone, she shuddered at the thought of the slow, fifteen mile-per-hour tour through the winding "village" streets, the driver's-side window gaping open, the unavoidable pity and curiosity. Wondered whether this would be the final deviation from the prosperous norm that provoked her openminded neighbors into judgment.

He colored more conspicuously. "Good God, you can't be frightened of me, can you?" And then: "No. No, I'm sorry. I shouldn't have said that. Of course you are." Though she hadn't replied. "It's understandable. You have no idea who I am. What kind of person I am." He ran a hand through his impeccably styled hair. "Stay here. I'll bring something out to you."

"I'm not frightened."

"Nonsense." He'd already turned. "It won't be five minutes."

Once he'd gone, she continued to glare at Thor. Holding up a strap of her bra with one hand, covering her chest with the other arm. The cat was already moving toward the truck. Agile, it leapt into the cab through the open driver's-side window, watching from inside as Talius returned with a cashmere sweater similar to the one he was wearing, but in a dusky pink rose.

Vivian slipped the sweater over her head, surprised by the tactile pleasure she took in the feel of the fabric against her bare skin. It reminded her of the lynx pushing its head against her belly. Its ear tufts moving across the surface of her neck and collarbone, when it was losing itself in her flesh.

Being dressed also made her feel braver. Annoyed by the nervousness she had shown, which had left the timid, privileged nonentity who was standing in front of her at a distinct advantage in their bizarre relationship. He clearly fancied her. If she allowed him to, perhaps he'd even help her out of her financial difficu—she killed the thought before it had formed. Though she was desperate, she was far from despicable. And she owed the man some quarter.

"I'm not frightened," she repeated. "I—I'd like to look at your roses. Those that I can see from here are extraordinary." She tried to summon up an intelligent question. "But they can't be in season, can they?"

"They're always in season." He stood to the side to let her through to the footpath.

"Oh." She glanced back at the cat, which hadn't moved from the cab of her truck. Gazing at them both, its complacent eyes half-closed, looking as though it had completed some trying task and would now have a well-deserved rest. She stepped

under the arched opening through the hedge.
Forced a smile at Talius.

"I'd love to have you for lunch," he said.

"Yes," she replied. "I'd like that too."

THE hedge of roses was higher and longer
than it had seemed from the outside. Walking
close beside Talius, smelling a whisper of his soap
or aftershave, understated and masculine but also
evocative of rose, Vivian couldn't make out any
part of the house. No hint even of an outbuilding.
All she could see, rising up on either side of her,
on occasion meeting overhead, on occasion
tugging at the threads of the cashmere sweater,
were twisted, thorny canes bearing hideous
cabbage roses that projected wave upon wave of
their own ominous, honeyed fragrance. The
atmosphere, despite the meticulous cultivation,
reminded her of Thor's forest at midnight, under
the canopy. She was growing frightened again.
Which irritated her.

But they did, despite her mounting and
irrational apprehension, eventually reach the
house. A palatial structure, where lunch was
already prepared. Two place settings at a small,
baroque-feeling wooden table in a bow window.
Not the dining room, she suspected. Nothing
ostentatious. Nothing in bad taste. Everything very
quiet and very expensive.

They ate venison. And Vivian was rude.
She couldn't help it. Talius's passivity provoked it
in her. She also found herself increasingly resentful

that she couldn't rid herself of demeaning thoughts about his wealth. He was pining for her. He was presentable. He could, in an instant, with a few strokes of a keyboard, elevate her from the squalor into which she had fallen. And she hated herself for dwelling on his usefulness. Hated him for being useful.

He poured them both glasses of wine from a bottle she ought to have recognized. Refused to recognize. He was unperturbed. She did, though, study, surprised, the stylized, gold lynx's head embedded at the base of the glass's stem. A family crest, perhaps. Or a business logo. Either way, it was a coincidence. He noticed her looking, but he didn't comment.

Instead, he poured her a second glass of wine, watching, pleased, as she drank. "I imagine you wonder what I do."

"No." She placed the empty glass on the table in front of her. Still rude. "No, I don't."

"Most of the time, I'm nothing more than an heir." Charmingly contrite.

"Hmm."

"But I've been diversifying recently." He watched her. "You see, I've developed an interest in strategic fiscal management."

She wondered for a stupid, hopeful moment whether he was offering her a job. Private financial advisor. Far less degrading than the contemptible fantasies she'd been entertaining before. She kept her voice neutral. "Why?"

"Ah." He lowered his gaze. "A bit of a crisis, in fact. A war of sorts." He paused. "An interloper began buying up my family's assets. Cut inroads into our property. Destabilized my hold on our real estate. I was uncertain about how to respond. And so, I took advice."

He already had an advisor. She lifted the glass to drink more wine, but it was empty. Set it down. "And?"

"This—predatory business concern," he said, "had begun, apparently, as a small hedge fund. Effective and successful, but nothing to threaten a position such as my own. Until something unusual—supernatural, even, said its competitors—triggered it into a flush of aberrant growth." He smiled. "Supernatural. Imagine that. An ogre of a hedge fund, yes?"

"Right. An ogre of a hedge fund."

"Anyhow, my advisors suggested that I run a few tests. Experiment with its managers to gauge their responses to market forces. To stresses and the like. Get a sense of the competition."

"That sounds reasonable." She was feeling lightly intoxicated. And, against her better judgment, she was enjoying the conversation. She'd missed her field of expertise. She wanted to say something brilliant to him, but she couldn't summon anything beyond the commonplace. "What did you do?" she asked instead.

"I followed their advice."

"And?" she repeated.

"First, I set out bait. Two or three empty shells of companies that appeared enticing. Wondering whether the fund was willing to grow. To shift into a holding company of sorts."

"Did it?"

"With a vengeance. And that, I fear, is where you met your fate, Vivian. I'd no idea it could—or sought to—grow so large."

Instantly, she was sober again. He knew about her previous life. "Is there something you want—" She tried to address him by name, but stumbled over the letters. Closed her mouth.

"Growth," he said, ignoring her question, "is relatively easy. Especially for a fund that's already of a certain size. Momentum does the trick more often than not. The true question, really, was whether a company of that size could shrink. Hide itself away, as it were."

"Take a defensive stance."

"Yes," he agreed. "A good way of putting it. Take a defensive stance. And so, I convinced a colleague of mine in the Treasury Department to startle them. Close up a few tax loopholes. Block escape routes."

"And?"

"Less than six hours later, it had dwindled to nothing. A little mouse hiding on a sliver of a Caribbean reef. Gone." He scrutinized his own wine glass. "But I was waiting for it there. And I gobbled it up. The entire concern is mine now. Problem solved."

She wanted to ask him what any of this had to do with her. With her work for the bank. With Thor, even. But she felt a wave of nausea and clapped a hand over her mouth instead. Closed her eyes. Too much wine.

"You look unwell," he said, standing to help her out of her chair. "There's a lavatory just upstairs. On the right. I'll wait for you here, and then we'll return you to your truck."

She swallowed and nodded. Her head had cleared, but she wanted to splash water on her face. Get herself into a proper state to drive. The cashmere sweater, which before had soothed her, felt clammy now. Clinging hot and tight like a bandage. She was itching to pull it off. To return to her sane, plastic townhouse. Away from all of this talk of growth and shrinkage.

As she climbed the carpeted stairway, her sneakers slicing a trail through the thick pile, she noticed more variations on the lynx motif. Carved into a dark wooden balustrade. Hidden in the pattern of the silk runner. At the edge of a stone mullion skirting the window above the top stair. Clearly a family tradition. Perhaps transferred to the businesses. Talius, she decided, was less passive than she'd believed. But she didn't like him any better. And she trusted him far less.

She dismissed the thoughts of Talius when she reached the corridor. Anxiety, as it always did, giving way to irritation. "On the right," she discovered, could be any one of fifteen anonymous closed doors. Stretching dimly toward a narrower wing of the house.

Annoyed, she tried the first. A wood-paneled room, empty aside from twenty or thirty metal filing cabinets, scattered haphazard across the floor. She closed the door. Moved to the next room. Opened the door. This room was brightly lit by sunshine, the menacing rose bushes cut away from its three large windows. But it was also full of caged birds, which began screeching and flapping violently against their bars when they sensed her presence. She slammed the door shut. Felt her nausea rise again. Chastised herself for her nerves and considered what to do next.

Though she knew mathematically that it made no difference whether she continued opening the doors in a sequence or skipped about, intuitively she dreaded experimenting with the third door. And so, gathering her wits, she traversed the hall and stood before the closed door at the end. Telling herself that the intelligent move would be to ignore it altogether, descend to the ground floor, thank Talius for his hospitality, and get herself back to her village. Lose the lynx in a different forest next time.

Nonetheless, steeling herself, she reached for the handle. Gripped it, twisted it, and opened it on silent, effortless hinges. The room was larger than the others. A sort of tower, or bower, with tall windows on three sides, letting in light filtered through a tangle of deep red Don Juan climbing roses.

But she could see little of the roses, or of the windows, because the room itself was stuffed to overflowing with rolls and swells of naked, pulsating flesh. And though she couldn't make out a face, hands, feet, or any identifiable body part or characteristic within the carnal excess, something silently screamed in her mind that the flesh was human. Despairing. There was also an overwhelming effluvia of powdered convenience store doughnuts and—though she didn't quite trust her senses—wet cash seeping from the thing's pores.

Without shutting the door, she whimpered and stumbled backward. Turned. Collided with Talius, who was standing behind her. He was taller than she'd remembered. He reached around her and opened the door wider. Whatever was in the room wouldn't be escaping via the corridor. Though it did spill out onto the floor.

"You've missed the lavatory," he said, pointing back down the hall. The third door was open. She could see a mundane sink and toilet.

She turned back to the bower. Asked the question. Unable to stop herself, though she knew that her curiosity was fatal. "What is it?"

"I've told you," he said. "I grow roses. I inherited this one from the ogre."

"The—ogre."

"Ogre of a hedge fund," he said. A joke. "Supernatural growth."

Then, cocking his head, he shoved his hand into a pillow of the flesh that was squeezed, an abraded crease, against the joint of the door. Extracted his hand with a foul sucking sound, gripping three or four sapphires, a cube of platinum, five or six hundred dollars in cash, and some sort of certified document. He held the document up to the light. "Interesting. I hadn't realized they'd gone public. Useful information."

He tossed the cash and jewels into a corner of the corridor and pocketed the certificate. Then, with a heave, he pulled the door to the tower room shut, using a foot to shove the excess flesh inside. Straightened his sweater.

Vivian, who had watched the scene unfold in cringing silence, took another step backward. Forced herself to keep from trembling. Looked him in the eye. "I don't need the sink. I'll go now. Thor will be—"

"Forgive me," he interrupted her. "But I'm afraid I can't let you go now that you've seen my roses."

Without replying, she turned toward the stairs. Confident that she could defend herself if he attempted to detain her by force. Talius was not a physically intimidating man. But before she took an additional step, the nausea returned, accompanied by a black dizziness. She thrust out an arm, which he took. Steadying her.

"It was in the wine," he said. Apologetic.

She shook off his hand. And then sat heavily on the carpet that ran the length of the corridor. Looked up at him. "But I drank the wine before I saw the roses." A stupid thing to say. She shut her eyes.

"Hmm." She could hear the smile in his voice. "Yes, I suppose you did."

With a heroic effort, she opened her eyes. Made one last attempt. "Talius." Good, she'd managed his name. "Talius, listen. If this is about my job—the bank—I can help you. I'll give you whatever information you want. I've got no loyalty to them. They left me with nothing. You needn't keep me here."

He laughed. "Oh dear, no. No, this has nothing to do with your job, Vivian." He chuckled again. "With your 'expertise.'" She felt him lifting her into his arms. Stronger than she'd have expected as well. "No. It's nothing like that."

He began walking with her toward another staircase. Further up into the house. Past other closed doors. "You're here because my cat likes you. That's all."

As he positioned her on a wide bed in a tower room that rivaled the chamber of the thing downstairs, she sensed, half asleep, half drugged, peach light dappling her body. The scent of roses. And then, moments later, the dead weight of the lynx stretched across her belly, pushing its head into her chest. A touch of drool. A needy and insistent cat.

Hops

THE maple tree was tall. Its leaves had unfolded, stretched, and taken on their mature candy-apple green. The branches, tangled, were a fluttering screen. And under ordinary circumstances, Jack would have felt safe leaning against the trunk, thirty feet above the forest floor. Invisible and concealed.

But he wasn't invisible. They could sense him even if they couldn't see him. He curled up against the peeling strips of ridged, grey bark, clutching the metal that covered the glass vial in his pocket, and watched the top of their bright blond heads circling beneath him. He wished he could burrow further into the bark. Lose himself inside the tree.

"We know you're up there." The voice came indistinct from the underbrush. The boy. The girl never spoke.

Jack remained silent. Watched as a bluebottle fly took three or four experimental steps across his hand and then, bored, flew off elsewhere. He held his breath.

"Look," said the voice. "My sister can chew through the trunk of that tree in a half hour if she wants to. Then you'll lose your hiding place for good. We don't want to hurt you."

Jack squeezed his eyes shut. Felt a sharp thud work its way up from the bottom of the tree. And then a monotonous chiseling sound. He opened his eyes. The girl was looking up at him. Gnawing at the tree. She could see him. He whimpered.

"We don't want to hurt you," repeated the boy. "Just come down so we can talk. There's something you can do for us. We've heard you're good at climbing."

Jack considered his options. The tree shuddered under the girl's onslaught. He had no options. Still clutching the vial's container in his pocket, he addressed the boy. "Tell her to stop. I'll come down."

The boy pulled the girl off the tree. Kissed the top of her head. She was very pretty, Jack thought to himself as he lowered himself to the ground. For a monster.

When he jumped down from the last set of branches, he stood before them. The boy was taller, and the girl shorter, than he was. But they were both pretty. And frightening. Jack continued to clutch the vial in his pocket. Hoping they wanted something else.

"What's in your pocket?" the boy asked.

Jack sighed. He withdrew his hand. Showed them the stoppered bottle in the metal container. "It's for my mother."

The boy and the girl looked at one another. Unfamiliar with mothers. "We need it. We heard you talking to the old man. It's precisely," said the boy, "what we need."

"I've told you," said Jack. "It's for my mother. She needs it more than you do."

The boy scrutinized Jack. Licked his lower lip.

Jack lowered his gaze. He couldn't run. He couldn't go back up his tree. Perhaps, he thought unconvincingly, his mother would understand if he lost it. "Why do you need it?"

"We'll show you." The boy and the girl began walking toward the edge of the forest.

After a second or two of hesitation, Jack ran after them.

They walked for ten minutes until the fir and cedar forest gave way to elderberry trees, and then to open meadow. Now, in July, the meadow grass was punctuated by furry white spears of mullein and yellow ragwort flowers. The sun felt visible. The heat shimmering.

The boy beckoned to Jack and pointed out a tall stone wall that cut across the center of the meadow. Obstructing chance passage. "He built it to keep the deer out of the kitchen gardens."

Jack nodded. Apprehensive. No one could climb that wall.

"Now he hides in there." The boy looked sidelong at Jack to be certain he was comprehending. The girl was lying on her stomach, chewing the petals off a Black-Eyed Susan flower. Her own eyes closed.

Jack nodded again. Swallowed.

"He's got something we want." The boy paused. "Something our father wants."

"I can't climb the wall." Jack had found his voice. He moved his shoe, nervous, as the girl, her eyes still closed, sniffled closer.

"You won't need to climb the wall." The boy beckoned again. "Look at this."

The three of them crept on their hands and knees, hidden beneath the bronze blades of grass, inhaling dry, fertile dirt, until they'd reached the base of the wall. It was thick. Solid. Twenty or more feet tall. Impenetrable.

But then Jack saw it. A muscular curl of some peacock-green stem had pushed through the mortar securing one of the foundation stones. From the other side. It was no more than an inch round, and it had extended only a foot or so beyond the wall and into the meadow. But it was strong. Greedy. Jack nudged it with a finger, which he quickly drew back when a tendril from the vine, or bine, encircled his hand and pulled in return. Slicing into a cuticle.

110

ON THE NATURE OF THINGS

Jack put his finger into his mouth, tasted blood, caught an appraising look from the girl, and then returned his attention to the boy. "What do you want me to do?"

"We heard you talking to the old man," the boy repeated. "The stuff in the bottle he gave you, it expands things."

"For my mother." Sullen. "In her lab."

Jack's mother was a marine biologist for the EPA. She and her team were engineering a bacterium that would eat plastic and then produce oxygen as waste. To combat the Great Pacific Garbage Patch, she told him, an oceanic region that had figured prominently in Jack's geography of the fantastic for as long as he could remember. Before Narnia. Before Middle-Earth. Before Gormenghast. Certainly before the dystopian bureaucracy staffed by those wizard schoolchildren with the implausible personal motivations. A mythical place.

He'd never told his mother that until quite recently, he'd wished every night that he himself might visit the Great Pacific Garbage Patch. A magical island swirling in an uncharted part of the ocean conjured together out of billions of bits and pieces of lives discarded and then reconstructed into something both baneful and mysterious. Until recently. He knew better now. The Great Pacific Garbage Patch was not an honorable adversary. No Lady of the Green Kirtle.

He'd never had a father. Though on the first Tuesday of every month, his mother left him alone in the house with a dinner of take-out Vietnamese food to attend her Single Mothers by Choice meeting. He looked forward to those evenings as opportunities to sneak into her basement lab to explore her bacteria. To fill a few test tubes with water and bubble tea.

This morning, though, she'd summoned him to the lab herself, to send him on an important errand. The obstacle that her team had encountered as they'd worked on their bacterium had been the size of the organism. Though it operated as they'd predicted, it reproduced with glacial slowness. Refused to grow. Remained tiny and, thus, could never match a foe like the Giant Garbage Patch.

Now, however, a colleague on the other side of the forest had discovered a promising genetic mutation that might be added to the mix. And so his mother, in the middle of a distillation she couldn't leave, had sent Jack out to retrieve the material for her. It might make all the difference, she explained to him. A vital mission.

Staring at his shoes, refusing to meet the blond boy's look under the shadow of the stone wall, Jack recalled the events of the morning. He'd felt the two following him once he'd left his mother's house. And when he'd entered Professor Spriggins's tiny cottage, adjacent to the Professor's own barn-like lab, he'd heard the rustling beyond the bewildering hay-bales. (Professor Spriggins owned no livestock.) But, preferring self-importance to disquiet, he'd ignored his

112

misgivings. Told himself not to ruin his quest. Refused to hear them.

Professor Spriggins, himself not the sort to notice anomalous environmental conditions, had bustled Jack into the lab, chattering about his discovery. A small, fussy elderly man with a face like a Corinthian owl sculpture, he believed, incorrectly, that children adored him. And so, he talked at them. Incessantly.

Jack had understood little of the monologue, aside from what his mother had already told him about the stuff in the vial making things bigger. But then, he also hadn't been listening very closely. Concentrating instead on not tripping over the piles of printed still shots from speculative, cryptozoological YouTube videos and copies of that dead geographical society's journal, long passages circled in excited red, that littered the floor. On ignoring the smell of condensed milk and unwashed tea towels. Condensed milk, perhaps, *on* unwashed tea towels.

Professor Spriggins had stoppered the bottle—a tiny thing, the size of Jack's smallest finger—sealed it, settled it into a foam cushion, placed the cushion into a metal container, snapped the container shut, and handed it to Jack. "Take it directly to your mother, Jack."

"Okay." Jack had stuffed the container into his pocket. Staring, petulant, at the Madagascar hissing cockroach that Professor Spriggins wore on his shoulder, as a pet. Unwilling to show his discomfort.

"Pet the cockroach?" Professor Spriggins had lowered his shoulder toward Jack.

Jack had taken an involuntary step backward. Overturning the pile of journals after all. Shaking his head.

"Straight back home, remember. Don't stop. Don't let the contents of that vial touch *anything* except your mother's bacteria." He'd been wearing an unreadable smile as he cautioned the boy. As though he'd known something that Jack never would.

Annoyed, Jack hadn't deigned to reply. Of course he wouldn't mess with the vial. He knew better. His mother's work was crucial. She was Saving the Earth.

But the moment he'd left Professor Spriggins's lab, he'd known something was amiss. He'd heard the footsteps again. No longer stealthy. Gaining on him. Following him into the forest. Inhabiting the forest with a confidence that he himself had never felt under the green-dark canopy. He'd seen their blond heads. And then he'd taken refuge, a final stand, in the maple tree. His maple tree.

NOW, gripping the container with the vial in his pocket, he recognized that he'd been defeated. The boy knew what it was. He wanted it. Jack had nowhere to run. He pulled the container from his pocket and handed it to the boy.

Without speaking, the boy knelt on the dry ground, opened the container, unwrapped the foam, and held up the vial. He removed the stopper. Sniffed, experimental. "It smells of condensed milk."

"I think that's from the lab," Jack muttered.
The boy considered. "How does it work?"
"I don't know."

The boy nodded, accepting Jack's answer. "I'll try just a drop on this leaf."

Jack nodded in turn. Perhaps if they didn't use all of it, he might still bring some home to his mother. Also, he was curious. He leant over and watched as the boy tipped a tiny, whitish teardrop onto a leaf. Just to the side of a curling stem, and between a pair of iridescent green cone-shaped flowers. Hops flowers, he thought irrelevantly. Odd in the middle of a deserted meadow.

For three or four seconds, nothing happened. But then, the leaf began to unfold and stretch, like a cramped hand released from some restriction or restraint. After that, the flowers swelled, shivering as though blown and pulled by a wind. And finally, the stem reacted. It expanded from a one-inch, pencil-like protrusion, cautiously questing beyond the wall, to a writhing wrist-thick pipe, and then to a colossal vomit-green trunk, crushed up against the stone that had constricted it.

When the plant had completed its transformation, a three-foot high opening had been punctured in the wall, through which Jack could see the vine, the bine, extending, a comic sea creature—beneath the Garbage Patch, perhaps— toward a collection of distant buildings. It stretched equally far back across the meadow and into the forest.

He addressed the boy. They had both taken a step back when the plant had begun to grow—the girl uninterested in the situation, eating her way through the Black-Eyed Susans. "It worked. Can I have my mother's material back now?"

The boy shook his head. "Sorry. Only after you've gone through."

"You never said anything about going through." Jack struggled to keep the waver from his voice. Especially in front of the girl. Though she was hardly paying attention. He moved his shoe again.

"There's something in there that we need. For our father." The boy, though implacable, wasn't bullying. He had no interest in Jack's emotions, one way or the other. No apparent understanding of Jack as anything aside from a means to an end.

"Why can't you do it yourselves?" Jack squinted, anxious, up at the setting sun. His mother would begin to worry soon.

"Because he knows us," the boy replied. "The man in there. He'll chase us away again."

"He can smell us." This from the girl. She was capable of speech after all, though her voice sounded like sawdust. Jack decided that he liked it.

"There's other stuff in there, too," the boy said. "Go ahead and take it. Things your mother might like."

116

"Not as much as she'd like her material," Jack shot back at him.

The boy said nothing.

Frustrated, Jack looked at the girl, who had turned her attention to a patch of white yarrow. Then he bent over and peered through the opening. The stem, once it had pushed through the wall, shot upward into a stand of silver birch trees. Most of the journey would be high above the buildings inside. Above the danger.

He straightened. Still without options. "All right. I'll do it. What do you want me to get for you?"

"It's a statue. A small sculpture. It looks a bit like a girl."

"It belongs to your father?" Jack asked. "The man in there stole it from him?"

"No." The boy seemed confused by the question.

Jack frowned.

"Our father saw it there once," the boy explained. "He wants it now."

They did, then, have a sense, if a twisted one, of filial duty. Jack understood. In a way. "Do you know where it is?"

"Only that the man sleeps with it. You must be careful."

Another quest. Jack nodded. And then, with nothing more to say, he pushed his way through the hole the stem had split in the wall.

THE passage through the stone barrier was longer and more stifling than Jack had expected it to be. Hunched in the dark, clumps of dirt and rock falling into his hair, he was forced, repeatedly, to disentangle himself from inquisitive vegetal cords that wrapped around his ankles, his fingers, and once, grimly, his throat. When he finally crawled from the hole into the dusky light, pulling himself along by leaves and hops flowers that, in turn, pulled back, he was hacking up small clods of mud from his lungs. And upon reaching the open ground, he lay, face down, breathing in the grass, thinking that he might simply spend the night there.

A sudden assault by a belligerent goat, its udders sore and swollen, changed his mind, sending him scrambling up the hempen brown trunk to the top of the grove of birch trees. Once there, taking a leaf from the girl's book, he ate a watermelon-sized hops flower. Surveyed the scene. Meadow. Overgrown kitchen gardens. Decayed outbuildings. And a larger complex in the distance. His target.

Much like the hole in the stone wall, the path to the largest of the buildings was longer—miles longer—than it had seemed from the outside. Though he could complete the journey almost entirely via the bine, many feet above the ground, it would be a daunting trek. The stem twisted in on itself, meandering in and out of the surrounding forest and over a road at one point, before plummeting, like the thick, frozen plume of some submerged water beast, into what looked as though it may once have been a restaurant.

He wasn't certain he had the stamina for that sort of climb. But he had no choice. And he was curious. And so, spitting dry strings of hops flower toward the ground below, he began to climb.

At first, the behavior of the plant was unusual enough to entertain him. It felt like a poorly trained pet, endearing almost in its eagerness to grip his ankles or send meddlesome tendrils up under his shirt and through his collar. Coiling itself occasionally, unbearably, in the blind alley of his armpit. But after an hour of pushing back feather-light leaves and hair-like stems, disentangling his feet and, once, frustrated, cutting through a fragile, thread-thin ringlet with his teeth— the plant had been shocked then, drawing into itself, quiet for ten or fifteen minutes—he became annoyed. The bine was tiresome. Jack feared he would fall.

He also realized as he moved further into the walled meadow that the enclosure wasn't as empty as he'd believed it to be. And when the stalk of the plant dipped close to the ground, he was forced on more than one occasion to hide from passers-by. Once, alarmingly, he'd nearly been spotted by two unhappy, elderly women in a Subaru. At that point, he'd curled himself into a knot in a crook of the stem, pulling a leaf, unexpectedly variegated, the size and feel of a green and white Kevlar sail, over his head, and waited. Trembling.

They'd gone their silent, disappointed way, and he'd crawled out from under the leaf only to come face-to-face with a small, stinking man and his dying dog. But the man worried Jack less than the women had. Like Professor Spriggins, the man was batty. And though he looked the boy in the eye with a distracted and provoking smile on his face, Jack could tell that the man saw something else there. Not a boy. Not a boy's eye.

And so, Jack had slowly, carefully, without breaking the man's gaze, backed himself into the upper reaches of the bine. Pleased when he was finally above the stench of the dog, which brought back to him the smell of bullies waiting in school toilets. Best avoided.

When he reached the wood and stone building at the center of the compound, darkness had fallen. But Jack could see through the breached wall from which the stem uncoiled that its interior was lit by candles. Candles resting on round, wooden tables. Each table scattered with two or three paper menus, wrinkled and caked with dust. As though awaiting patrons who had never, would never, come.

The structure was also empty. And at its center was a platform, or dais, upon which a small, bluish, wrinkly statue stood. The object after which the blond boy had sent Jack. The key to retrieving his mother's vial.

ON THE NATURE OF THINGS

Keeping himself open to the noise or smell of the owner's return, Jack squeezed himself through the crack in the wall, hung by his fingertips from the bine, and then dropped to the floor. Gagged on the fetid air. The room smelled of fermentation. But a horrid fermentation—beer and yeast, yes, but also meat and anger and despair. He thought he also caught a hint of sausages going wrong, but he didn't want to breathe in deeply to confirm his suspicion. He removed his shirt and wrapped it around the lower part of his face. The room was warm enough, humid and stifling enough, to go naked.

Once he'd reconciled himself to the environment, Jack took a few timid steps toward the sculpture. Uncertain as to how he ought to carry it back with him. Though it wasn't overly large, it would be an ungainly burden. Difficult to push back up through the gap in the wall and then along the miles of playful, overexcited bine. He thought he might wrap it in his shirt and wear it on his back like a rucksack.

He moved closer to the base of the pedestal. Tilted his head. It was a strange object to have caught the attention of the boy's father. Unquestionably a little girl. Perhaps his own age. A bit older. He could see the facial features and the approximate shape of the body. Dressed for winter. A heavy coat and hat. Uncomfortable looking shoes. Jack felt an urge to remove the shoes, which he pushed down, embarrassed. A strange reaction. And, most bewildering, she appeared to be attached by strings to a loaf of bread.

Jack shrugged. He knew from his mother, who was broad-minded, that different people preferred different sorts of art. The boy's family must be progressive. The question that remained was how to move the thing from the pedestal to the plant, and then back to the stone wall.

Doubtful, he extended a tentative hand toward the figure's leg. Brushed its toe and then, drawing in his breath, retracted his fingertips. It felt wrong. Living. He knew, though he couldn't have said how, that the girl was freezing. Dying of cold, despite the oppressive clamminess of the room. She was also hungry. Famished. Carved out until she was empty, hollow, inside.

Jack raised embarrassed eyes to the girl's. He saw hopelessness. And, worse, he saw resignation. She had accepted her position on the dais, in this squalid inferno. She wished for nothing more.

So absorbed was he in the sculpture's spellbinding face, that he heard the man's return only when it was too late. And the filthy, matted legs were already crunching down the room's stairs when Jack registered that he must hide himself. But the room, though dim, candlelit, and scattered with chairs and tables offered no secure bolt hole. Behind the bar was too obvious. And there were no back exits. He was trapped.

Until the sculpture—although that was impossible, it couldn't have—showed him a way out. Transmitting knowledge to him of a low door embedded in a far corner of the room. Jack shook his head as he dropped to the floor and pulled himself along on his stomach toward salvation. He'd become suggestible during the exhausting climb. He must have registered the door subconsciously upon entering the room and then convinced himself that the girl had magically aided him. The sculpture was a sculpture. An object. A creepy object at that.

However he discovered the door, it saved Jack. He'd just crouched through and closed it behind him when the man reached the base of the stairway. Once inside, he examined the small room in the candlelight that streamed through a crack—bashed open in some recent rage, it seemed—in the wood.

Four tall, narrow walls. Sporting shelf after shelf of cheese, beer, and candles. Limited run cheese. Locally crafted beer. Hand-made candles. Jack knew intuitively that these were the sort of specialty products that his mother adored, but never purchased for fear of something she called "extravagance." He stuffed as many as he could into his pockets before turning, kneeling before the crack in the door, and peering at the man.

"What the fuck is that smell?" The man was shouting at the sculpture. As though he blamed it for something. "Is it a kid? A little friend of yours? If it is, I'll fucking eat him for lunch."

Jack, though terrified, was also perplexed. How the man could smell anything above the putrid meat and yeast was a mystery to him. But smell it the man did. For he lowered himself into a squat and began half-crawling throughout the room, sniffing at corners and floorboards. Unerringly, he was zeroing in on Jack's hiding place.

Holding his breath, Jack forced himself to keep watching. The man was verminous. Barefoot and bare chested, naked aside from a ripped shred of what might once have been cargo shorts, he scratched at the brown, matted hair that covered his back, chest, and legs. His beard, wild and unkempt, was caked with pieces of food—dried egg, sprigs of dill, smears of cheese (Jack resolved not to tell his mother), and the bones of a small animal. A pigeon, perhaps.

Tattoos ran across wide swaths of his skin, beneath the hair, but one in particular—a blurred face etched into his calf—was in a sorry state. Seeping blood, pus, and something black and flaking, it was obviously dangerously infected. The man dragged the leg behind him, unwilling to put weight on it. Jack found himself pitying the man. Though the pity didn't weaken his fear. The man was less than two feet away from the door, sniffing and grunting, laughing to himself.

"I've got you, you little—"

But then, above the infected stink of the man, above the rancid sausages—definitely, Jack decided, sausages—above the aging beer, and even above the small room's aroma of goats and

124

beeswax, came a wave of pure, intense yeast. The man went still and silent. Sniffed the air. Smiled.

"That's the stuff." He turned on his heel and crawled back toward the sculpture. Rested his head on the carved, wooden feet. "More."

Another wave of yeast saturated the room. The man closed his eyes. Sighed. Settled himself. And then began breathing deeply and heavily.

Jack waited for ten restive minutes. Before, cautious, he opened the pantry door and ventured into the candlelit room. Approached the sculpture again. In addition to propping his head on its feet, the man was clutching its thin ankles. His knuckles white with exertion.

Chewing his lip, Jack circled the pedestal. Gazed up at the thing's face. It looked amused. A girl who enjoyed the discomfiture of others. Jack lowered his eyes. Decided that he preferred the blonde one with the eating problems. This thing was baffling.

And, in any case, there was no chance of removing it from under the man's possessive grip. At least not tonight. Checking to be certain that he'd secured his mother's cheese, beer, and candles in his pockets, he pulled himself up onto the muscular green bine. Swatted away a sprightly, deadly, tendril. And climbed, cringing, because he was certain, despite his hectoring, rational argument to the contrary, that the girl—the thing— was laughing at him as he fled.

IT was not yet midnight when he emerged, exhausted, from the crumbling orifice in the stone wall. A gibbous moon, recently risen, had turned the dry meadow to shadowed chrome. The mullein spikes to skeletal shafts in some ancient graveyard. Jack shivered.

The boy and girl were waiting for him. The girl was curled into a tight ball, hot and flushed, sleeping and smiling as though dreaming of eating something satisfying. The boy, his face blank, bone-white, was sitting cross-legged beside her, a steadying hand on her round shoulder. When he saw Jack, the boy stood, mindful not to disturb his sister.

"Have you got it?" The boy's voice was doubtful. He could see that Jack was empty-handed.

"I saw it," Jack said. "I—I don't think it wanted to leave."

The boy nodded. He appeared to understand. But he remained uncompromising, nonetheless. "I'll keep the vial, then. Unless you want to try climbing in tomorrow—"

"No." Jack spoke over him. "No, it isn't worth it." He thought for a moment. "I did get goat cheese for my mother. And a candle. Real beeswax. So, it's all right."

"I'm glad," the boy said. Then he also paused, pensive, for a moment. "I like what the stuff in the vial does. It's better than the sculpture. Father—" He hesitated. Resumed: "Father doesn't know *what* he wants much of the time. He's a man of weak character."

"I haven't got a father," Jack offered. He was unsettled by the boy's cold, adult appraisal. The silver-white meadow. The grassy smell of the sleeping girl.

The boy's face didn't change. But then, after a few seconds: "it's late. Would you like us to help you find your way home? We know the forest well."

Jack turned his gaze to the writhing trunk of the vine—the bine—that stretched now from the edge of the stone wall past the elderberry trees and into the shadowed wood. Though unsettled, he realized that he was no longer frightened. He shook his head. "No, thank you. I'll follow the vine." He risked a quick smile at the boy. "It likes me. I think."

"Okay." The boy knelt beside the girl and began shaking her. Gently. "Thank you for trying, at any rate."

"No worries." Jack settled the palm of his hand against the rough, green trunk of the hops bine and allowed it to lead him toward the wood. Into the dark. He was looking forward to the quiet.

When he reached his house, a thin spray of stems now spiraling up and over the metal glider on their porch, his mother was waiting for him. Wearing pyjamas and holding a cup of cocoa. Not one given to displays of emotion, she kissed his head as he walked through the door, but otherwise she didn't react to his disheveled appearance.

"It's late, Jack. I was worried about you."

"Sorry, mother." He decided it would be easier to tell her everything immediately. "I was looking for your material. I'm afraid I lost it somehow. And I thought I could retrieve it. So I stayed out late. But—but it turned out that I couldn't get it back. I'm sorry," he repeated.

"I was more concerned about you than about my material." She handed him the cocoa. "And Professor Spriggins told me what had happened anyway. He brought over a second vial three hours ago. Told me he'd seen you at The Liquid Loaf, searching for it. You shouldn't have gone so far."

Jack frowned. And then, quashing his confusion, he returned to placating his mother. "I didn't go in, mother. I promise—"

"Of course you didn't go in. You're a minor. They wouldn't have let you in." She considered. "I believe they've closed down anyway. Funny place."

He reached into his pockets and produced the rounds of cheese, the candle, and the bottle of beer. Arranged them on their small dining table. An offering. "I did bring you these. I thought you'd like them. I *am* sorry about your material."

She lifted a packet of the cheese and examined it. Two goats doing something anthropomorphic. Dancing, perhaps. Playing pan pipes. "Where did you find them?"

"At the restaurant." He dropped his gaze and sipped his cocoa.

"They were having a sale? Going out of business?"

"Yes," he confirmed. "A sale."

She returned the cheese to the table. Lifted the candle. Sniffed it. "Goodness. What a smell." She kissed the top of his head again. "My favorite. Thank you, Jack."

"You're welcome, mother."

MUD

HELLO."

It was the odd girl. Seventeen years old, give or take. She crouched at the edge of the bridge that crossed the swamp behind the Institute. Wearing wet, mismatched socks. No shoes. Orange basketball shorts. Or perhaps they were orange men's underwear. A white t-shirt with an advertising slogan, misspelled, across the front. People who passed her looked in the other direction. Embarrassed.

Those familiar with the neighborhood knew that she was not seventeen, but precisely two decades old. Adopted twenty years ago from a fashionable African or perhaps Southeastern European country. A country in the news. Difficult to recall which. Her adoptive parents had raised five healthy boys of their own, and they'd wanted to give back.

Three or four years later, when the African or Southeastern European country had dropped from the news, the girl had disappeared as well. No one knew what had become of her. No one had noticed or cared. Until four or five years after that, when she'd reappeared under the bridge. A decade old. Speaking an incomprehensible composite of English and Latin, something that may have been Balkan, and something almost certainly African. A hint of old Scandinavian. Vowels and guttural glottal clicks. Burbling.

The spine-curdling quality of the girl's language, however, was less that it was incomprehensible than that it was on the verge, on an agonizing knifelike edge, of meaning. Reminiscent not only of communication, but of communication that—if missed—would do the listener unthinkable harm. Those who crossed the bridge strained to hear, to understand the girl. But they couldn't. And when they reached the other side, they found themselves bereft. Mourning some bloodied chunk of their soul that the girl had taken from them. Had hidden away in the black swamp muck beneath the frayed wood and metal struts.

The shrewder of the girl's victims would offer her a coin to let them pass. Sometimes a bit more. But it did no good. They crossed diminished as well. And the more enlightened would speak to her in schoolroom Spanish.

Cosmopolitan. Displaying their appreciation of her intersectional positionality. That also did no good. True, the girl would respond. In her babble. But then, surging out of the global mix, would burst a clear, lacerating line of Ovid. Something, perhaps, about exile.

When the girl was twelve, and the bridge had become impassible by all but those seeking punishment or oblivion, the town had sent Social Services to collect her. Find her a proper home. An education. Social Services had never returned. The bridge remained quiet, damp, and dark. Dripping sludge and what no one wanted to accept as viscera.

Three years later, when she was fifteen, they'd sent Animal Control. Animal Control had also disappeared. An empty truck. An unfortunate raccoon half asleep behind wire. And a slow, single bubble breaking on the black surface of the water. A tranquil wetland.

Now, five years after that, Ash, thirty years old, wearing hiking boots and a fleece, stood at the far end of the bridge. Carrying a tranquilizer gun and, absurdly, a net. He suspected that neither would serve him well, and so he set them on the muddy ground at his feet. Maintained eye-contact with the girl.

"Hello," he replied to her as he straightened.

She responded with something high and nasal. A scrap of an Eddic poem, he sensed. She narrowed her eyes, sensing in turn that he'd

132

identified the tag. Regrouped and shouted something produced at the front rather than the back of her mouth, rippling across her teeth and then across the bridge. Catullus. Without a doubt.

He remained silent, watching her, not acknowledging the babble. He loathed languages. The useless education that had landed him a job as the bitch in a private investigative firm run by two senior partners who clearly wanted him dead. If not, why send him on this assignment? Take care of the suburban troll, they'd said. Liberate the rich women and their bridge. Kill the guilt.

The girl, cocking her head, tried a few more words. These he didn't recognize. Something African, he thought. From the east or the south. His education had gone only so far.

Registering his blank reaction, the girl's lip curled in ugly contempt. But she was an ugly thing generally. Squat torso. Abnormally long, withered arms. Something wrong with the skin that showed through the drying mud and the orange shorts. A snail's track of clotted green mucus hanging from one thin nostril.

Having stumped him, she began to sink beneath the dirt and metal at the other end of the bridge. Satiated. While Ash felt a sharp, cold thumbnail of despair or guilt or misery work itself into his chest, where it scraped and dug at what the reptilian part of his mind recognized as his soul. He gasped. Clutched, involuntary, at his heart.

And then, gathering his wits, he shouted across the bridge. Swahili. He'd studied a bit back when he'd cared. The only African language he knew. A cliché, but perhaps it would stop the girl's descent. He needed more from her than contempt if he was going to complete his assignment. He needed an invitation. Prior to rooting her out of her lair.

The girl halted her plunge. Twisted her smile in a different direction. Speculative. Beckoned to him with a thin hand disfigured by red and abraded knuckles. "Come into my parlor?"

"Uh—yes. Thank you." He hazarded a few steps onto the rotting planks of the half-submerged bridge. "This way?"

"No. Under." The girl dove beneath the sludge.

Ash sighed inwardly, unsurprised by the turn the conversation had taken. And then, resigned, he lowered himself into the cool muck of the swamp. Waded waist deep in the direction of the puddle she'd recently occupied. Saw the piles of dead leaves and decaying plastic at a dry edge that indicated a rodent's warren. Too large for a rodent. The girl's home. He pushed through after her. At least he wouldn't be swimming.

The girl's hole was cleverly constructed— lofty beneath the dripping decay of the swamp, yet invisible to even the most diligent of searchers. Otherworldly. Aristocratic, almost, in its rejection of suburban comfort.

But it was also unlivable to any being accustomed to space and air. Ash found himself clutching at the roots of wetland plants that punched through her roof and walls. Willing them to lead him to the surface. Away from the crushing matter—the heaps and piles of things and objects and bulk that cluttered the girl's home, material manifestation of her garbled, insistent language. Her muddied language.

But he said nothing. Instead, he followed her through a dirt antechamber massed with loose pages of books and journals that had been smeared into illegibility by a uniform reddish muck. From her fingers or from bleeding knuckles perhaps. Spittle. It was impossible to tell, and he didn't want to know. Paid little attention.

When they'd passed through the antechamber and reached the vaulted hall that served, he supposed, as the girl's living space, she lit a stub of a beeswax candle with a Marine Corps cigarette lighter. Turned back to him. Spoke to him in immediately recognizable French. Baudelaire. *Aimer et mourir au pays qui te ressemb—* She was giving him a gift. An easy one.

He forced a smile. Gagged back his horror at the space. At the foul girl. At her weeping skin sores and mucus. At the piles of bones and coins and fecal matter and food debris and gold that littered the floor. At the walls spackled with layer upon layer of paper scraps that were written over and taped together into an organic-feeling mass.

The girl caught him looking at the oddments of paper. Beckoned him closer. Pointed at a beige piece with rough edges that looked as though it had been chewed. Sucked into wet threads.

"My words," she said.

"Yes," he agreed.

"From the bridge. I take their words. Then they're my words." She frowned and indicated a cardboard box sagging under the weight of greasy dimes and pennies. Reeking of filthy circulation. "I take their coins."

He nodded, uncertain as to what she was trying to communicate to him.

Frustrated, she muttered a few lines of what may have been Russian. Old Slavonic. Something. Then she indicated the fecal matter. "I take their souls."

"That," he said, experimenting with an argument, "is shit."

"Yes," she agreed in turn. No argument.

Pensive, she rammed a jagged fingernail into a nostril. Removed what she found and rubbed it along her lower lip. "Look at my words."

Ash didn't need encouragement. Any excuse not to look at the girl herself. He took a polite step toward the slips of paper affixed to one another and then to the wall. "Mud," he read on one. "*Laspi.*" He blinked. Read further:

eabar
ts'ekh
fango
blato
søle
mwd

labou
lokatz...

The list continued. Hundreds of tiny bits of paper. Thousands. Encroaching upon one another. Making a fluttering tapestry of the chamber. Swarms of pulpy moths. Breeding. Doing unspeakable things in the dark.

"I like mud," she said.

"Why?" he hazarded.

"Safe."

Fair enough. He frowned at the shadowed chamber, considering his next move. Though he was pleased to have infiltrated the girl's lair, and more than pleased that his viscera weren't yet decorating the bridge, he couldn't determine how he'd convince her to depart the area. Or, if that wasn't possible, how he'd level her hole. He knew that he'd never find it again without her permission, and she wouldn't grant him permission unless he won her trust. If there was only something he could offer her. A bargain. Her kind liked that sort of thing.

First, however, he must keep the conversation going. Catching the glint of something brilliant blue and valuable at the edge of a dirt wall, he squinted into the gloom. Yes. Sapphires. Jewels of every conceivable size and quality. Along with what he thought might be legal documents. The yellowing deeds to properties? Resort hotels. Casinos. He pointed. "What's that?"

"Mother." Her voice tired.

He waited for her to elaborate, but she seemed disinclined. After a few more seconds, he scratched his head and returned to the center of the chamber. "Oh."

"Will you eat?" The girl's eyes, large and bloodshot, were downcast.

Ash nodded, reluctant.

The girl pointed to a stack of sodden newspaper, thirty years old, tied with a frayed bit of yellow, plastic twine. "Sit. I'll bring water."

Ash balanced himself on the newspaper. His knees high. His hands clasped between his legs. Watched as the girl tied a pink apron about her lumpen waist. Kittens having a barbecue. Watched as she retrieved an old plastic soda bottle from another cardboard box, a shred of the original Dr. Pepper label still in place. The brown dregs of what he prayed wasn't Dr. Pepper at the bottom. Watched as she tied back her mangy hair with a wire twist-tie.

And then continued to watch, in paralyzed disbelief, as, with a running start, she rammed her face with full force against a stone part of the wall. Backing up, she ran at the wall again. And again. And again. Until Ash, gathering his wits, leapt from the stack of newspapers to stop her.

Confused, she looked up at him. There was a bump the size, shape, and color of an overripe fig in the center of her forehead. Above her greasy nose. And something far more than a trickle of blood gushed down her face, bubbling over her lips and chin. She extended an experimental tongue and tasted the effluvia. "What?"

"What the hell are you doing?"

She held up the plastic soda bottle. "Getting water."

"That's insane."

"Have some?" She rummaged about in a child's plastic cupboard until she found a sippy cup. Thirty-year-old images of Popeye the Sailor eating a tin of spinach. Pushed it at him.

He took it, and she poured him nonexistent water from the empty soda bottle. Then she stood back and watched, blood still dribbling down her forehead, to be certain that he drank. Holding the cup between a thumb and index finger, he mimed sipping.

"Lips," she said.

Forcing down the taste of bile, he pressed the top of the cup against his mouth and pretended to drink. Placed the cup on the mud floor beside his foot. Watched her in turn.

"Good?"

"Yes," he said. "Very good. Thank you."

"Now have some fish."

He returned to the stack of newspapers and lowered himself onto it. Suspicious. Playing along because he could think of no other way to gain her trust. To discover a method of ejecting her from under the bridge.

She turned away from him and crawled through a hole that led, he assumed, to a storage area. He heard her mumbling to herself.

139

Something Slavic again. Her preferred language group, he suspected.

Five minutes later, she returned with a used paper plate, a large spot of brown grease at the center, on which she'd placed a small, yellow fish. Made of rubber. A child's bath toy. He could just make out the features of a popular animated character from ten or eleven years before faded from one end of it. Staggering a touch—blood loss, no doubt—she flourished the plate in front of him and set it to his side.

"Eat."

"It's a plastic toy."

She muttered again. Iambic pentameter. But vocabulary he couldn't identify. Then she pointed. "Eat."

"I think," he said standing, "that I'll pass this time. Thank you nonetheless. I'm grateful to you for having invited me—"

"You eat the fish," she said, "and you return tomorrow. With the book."

He blinked. "The book?"

"Yes. I take the book. I leave." Her face moved, but he couldn't tell whether she was smiling with the blood running over her mouth. "Problem solved."

Holding her eyes, he sat once again on the stack of newspapers. Reached for the yellow fish. Raised it to his lips and took a bite. Chewed. Swallowed. Another bite. And another. Altogether, it took him ten minutes to choke down the toy fish. But he kept it in his stomach. And when he was certain he'd continue to keep it inside of him for at least his journey home, he stood. "It was delicious. Thank you."

The girl mumbled something that might have been "hospitality," and then, to his horror, pushed a dirty hand down the front of her gritty white t-shirt. Explored her own flabby chest for a few moments, an enraptured expression on her face, and then pulled out a paperboard card. Small and folded. Thrust it at him.

He took it between his fingertips and held it up in the candlelight. A remnant from an ancient library card catalogue. A book in Old Norse. He shoved the card into his pocket. "Thank you."

"That book," she said. "Local library. A useful place. I take the book, I leave the bridge. Understood?"

He nodded.

"Good. Go."

THE town's public library was a clean, prosperous establishment, a modern, glass erection well supported by the charitable contributions of its patrons. And when Ash presented the librarian with the brittle, yellowing card, she was as affably intrigued by it as she was bemused. It was the work of five minutes to correlate its information with that in the online catalogue and to locate the volume he sought. Large and leather. Old. Valuable. He felt a pang of guilt that he'd be stealing it.

"I had no idea this was here," she said as she hefted it onto a carrel desk for him. Surrounded on three sides by blue and green bubbled glass. Recessed lighting. A potted swiss cheese plant. Monstera deliciosa. Like an overdesigned urban hotel.

"Thank you for taking the time to find it for me," he replied, meek. Meek worked best.

"Of course!" Bright and professional. "Let me know whether there's anything else you need."

"I will. Thank you again."

He dropped his eyes to the volume to avoid prolonging the exchange. His stomach still roiled from having vomited up pieces of rubber yellow bath toy throughout the previous night. He didn't want pleasant conversation. He wanted to end this assignment, collect his payment, and begin searching employment listings. Surely someone was in the market for languages. Someone must want his skills. He rubbed the palm of his hand across the stubble on his chin. Or not. Likely not. And at the moment, he must concentrate on the book.

It was, as the card had indicated, composed in Old Norse. A dialect that annoyed him slightly less than many of the others he'd collected on his travels. And when he opened it to scan a few lines, familiarizing himself with the scribe's style, he established that it was straightforward. A variation on a medieval bestiary. Entertaining and educational. But, he confirmed as he continued to overturn thick, stiff pages, restricted to trolls. Trolls

142

of all types. Cave trolls, mountain trolls, friendly trolls, hostile trolls. No wonder the girl was interested.

He himself was not. In fact, the content of the book struck him less forcefully than did its tactility. His fingertips thrummed wherever they brushed the leather binding or the crumbling pages. The edges of the parchment. And the smell of the thing was heady. Overpowering. The skin of animals centuries dead. Salt from oceans that had long run dry. Ink that discharged wave upon wave of the metallic tang of blood. Brown ink. Mixed with the blue of rare Portuguese herbs, the black of wasps, gallnuts, and forest fires and the yellow of Iberian crocuses. Verdigris and lapis.

So entranced was he by the book's physicality under his hands, that he scarcely noticed when he reached the entry on Enchanted Trolls. Until he saw the images. A story in pictures. The story of a thing, an abomination, stinking and diseased, stretched of limb and swollen of abdomen, enormous teeth, released from its bondage. Transformed into a woman.

The illustration of the liberated troll extended over an entire otherwise blank page. Ash's breath was shallow as he ran his fingertip over her gold-dust hair, curling and twisting beyond the page's margin and border, a lock of it twined around the initial letter of the ensuing entry. On Mud Trolls.

He stared into her sapphire eyes. Which stared back out at him. Alive. Not of the page. Not lapis. More valuable than lapis. An herb not yet discovered, rediscovered, by modern chemistry. He traced the graceful curve of her delicate fingertip and wrist, creamy white. Rose petals.

The sole line of text, on the facing page, was a command: Eat with it. Lie with it.

He closed the book. Set his elbows on the edge of the carrel's desk and pressed his fists into his eyes. The girl didn't want him to bring her the book. She wanted him to liberate her. He'd already eaten with her. And this, now, was the bargain she proposed in return for releasing the bridge. Lie with her.

Though the book was shut and his eyes closed, the rose gold image of the woman danced bright against the black light. He dropped his hands from his face. He'd present the book to the girl that evening.

ASH approached the civilized end of the bridge as the sun was setting. Though little sunlight permeated the miasmic gloom of this part of the swamp even at highest noon. The girl was waiting for him. Draped over a half-decayed strut, one fungal toe dipped in the brackish damp. Chewing the end of a lock of hair, which was either matted or inexpertly plaited.

When she saw him, she straightened and scratched at her head with a sharp fingernail. The chunk of hair she'd been chewing peeled from her scalp and splashed into the water. The girl stared down at it, perplexed, and then returned her attention to Ash. He held up the leather volume. Shrugged a silent question at her.

The girl beckoned to him once again and slid under the oily slick of swamp mud. He held the book above his head, waded in after her, and located her hole. Took a last breath of clean—cleanish—air and descended into her lair. Ignored the gold and the shit, concentrating instead on his strategy once he'd reached the largest of the caverns.

When he emerged into the relative openness of her living space, he saw that she'd attempted to tidy it. The more menacing piles of bones and food waste had been shoved into a far corner, and eighteen beeswax candles flickered in holders on the walls. Not too near the flammable paper. His confidence grew.

She turned to face him across the room and tossed him a few shy lines of Syriac. Her eyes downcast. Almost charming. Syriac, one of his first languages, came more than easily. Smiling in earnest, warm and interested, he replied. She raised her eyes and held out her hand.

"My book."

"Yes," he said, his voice now also warm. "Your book."

She blinked. Confused that he wasn't handing it to her. She took a step toward him. "I take the book. I leave."

"Yes." He moved closer. Perhaps this evening wouldn't be as agonizing as he'd believed. He was almost looking forward to it.

Sensing that she'd failed to communicate her meaning, the girl stopped. Frowned at the book in his hand.

And Ash, reminding himself to proceed gently, placed the book on the mud floor behind him. Best not distract her. He reached out to touch the girl's shoulder.

The girl stiffened at his touch and gaped at him with baffled, frightened eyes. Then she crouched into a squat and tried to scuttle around him to the book. Reaching out to it with her abnormally long, jointed fingers.

But he was too quick for her. Holding her under both of her outstretched arms, he lifted her to her feet and pushed her against a paper-smeared wall. Gazed into her face. Appreciated the sebaceous seepage from her pores, the pus-covered wound to the side of her mouth, her bloodshot eyes and her protuberant, chipped brown teeth. A few pieces of the paper fluttered to the floor.

"My words," she said. Bending toward the scraps.

He caught her by a gaunt wrist, twisting and tightening her slack skin. "Forget them. Concentrate on this. On now."

"My book," she said.

He could feel her heart beating. And so, leaning forward, closing his eyes, he kissed her. Pressed his lips against her cracked, festering mouth. Forced her teeth apart and sought her tongue. Surprised himself by beginning to enjoy it.

146

ON THE NATURE OF THINGS

She tasted of things that thrive in the wet. Of shy, dangerous, hidden things encountered only once. Of bogs and silence. He wanted to appreciate it. To appreciate her.

But she also, he quickly realized, moved like a wet thing. Slippery and desperate. Mimicking the flopping anguish of something accustomed to depth and darkness forced into the sunlight, onto dry land. She was pushing back against him with all her strength. Straining to close her mouth, to expel his tongue. Making an unattractive squealing sound.

"Stop fighting it," he murmured into her ear. Long, distended, and caked with a mustard-colored encrustation. "This is for you. You needn't live like this. You can be so much more. I can help you."

"My book!" she shrieked once he'd released her mouth.

"I read your book," he reassured her. "I understand."

She spat a gob of greenish yellow spittle into his face. "I take the book. I leave."

Wiping the scum from the edge of his eye and his cheek, he nearly lost his resolve. But then, reminding himself that he was doing her a favor, he shoved her to the ground. He heard the back of her head crack against stone, worried for a moment, recalled the scene with the "water," and told himself that she'd already done far worse to herself on her own. Then, straddling her weakly twitching body, he pulled off the orange shorts.

Left the mismatched socks and the t-shirt. He had no interest in whatever she was hiding under the advertising slogan.

As she whimpered and stretched, clawing, for the book, he used his hands to push apart her thighs. Ignored the sweat and slime that coated his fingertips and palms as he sought an opening. Breathed through his mouth. Guarding himself against the stench of open sewers and rotting flesh that assaulted his senses. Then he shut his eyes once again, unzipped his trousers, and penetrated her. Repeatedly. Enjoying it once more. Despite himself. The girl went silent and frozen.

When he'd finished, he collapsed on top of her, no longer repelled by the smell or the feel of her. He liked the stink of decay. The spongy-sweet stickiness of fungus and filth. He pressed his nose against her damp neck and breathed her skin. Replete.

The girl, however, understanding that what had happened to her was now over, pushed him away. Backed, half-huddled, to the far wall. Hugged her knees and keened. Babbled to herself in a language that Ash had never dreamt of, much less studied or learned.

Surprised by her reaction, he sat up as well. Confused. Zipped his fly. Peered into the darkness to observe the transformation.

But there had been no transformation. All he could see was the odious, misshapen thing, unchanged and shuddering, a trail of snot and blood daubed across the floor—of course, she'd been a virgin—and a gaping wound at the back of her head, missing a patch of hair, where he'd pushed her down. Her orange shorts were crumpled, small and sad, on the other side of the room. She made no move to cover herself.

He stood, perplexed. Began to step toward her, reconsidered, and rubbed his cheek. "Does it take effect later? Gradually, maybe? Like in a few days?"

She stared into empty space, her rheumy yellow eyes wide and her putrid mouth a tragedy mask's black "o." An animal noise emanated from deep inside her throat. Inhuman. A troll's sound.

Ash flushed. Felt a tinge of remorse. And then, trying to hit upon means of remedying the situation, he remembered the book. Crossed the room, retrieved it, and set it in front of her. Three or four feet away. "There's your book."

She screeched something incomprehensible at him. Shook her head, shaking and hysterical. He backed up and blinked, annoyed now. How could she not understand that he'd been trying to help her? He watched her, as puzzled now as she'd been when he'd kept the book from her.

But then, coming to himself, he remembered his assignment. His reason for being here. The girl's bizarre reaction was irrelevant.

He cleared his throat. "As I said, there's your book. You gave your word to leave if I brought it to you. I've brought it to you. Our bargain stands. The bridge is free."

The girl, gathering about her the fragments of her aristocratic contempt for all things human, stood as well. Naked from the waist down, aside from the mismatched socks. And then, raising her arms, she pointed at him with both hands and spoke five words. Five words in a language older than speech. Older than communication. Something primordial and annihilating.

In the silence that followed, Ash felt the thumbnail that had grazed his soul on the bridge return, rushing and singing, in the form of a colossal and rusted sickle. Assaulting him. Gouging out all that he had inside of him. Leaving him hollow. Unmanned. Its sharp edge working on and on, hacking and cutting, until he knew that he would die.

But the invisible blade retracted itself after no more than three minutes. An exquisite and agonizing three minutes, but three minutes only. After which, the work of the words complete, he realized that he was still standing. Still breathing. Still intact. The only aftereffect a void-like melancholy. An anxiety that he'd lost something, he wasn't certain what, that he ought to recover, but couldn't think how.

Along with the realization that the girl's collection of fecal matter had grown into something towering and unbearable, and he must, immediately, leave. Holding his hand over his nose and mouth, Ash lurched backward and made for the surface of the swamp. One eye, cautious, watching the girl.

ON THE NATURE OF THINGS

But the girl didn't try to stop him. She made no move to extract his viscera. Rather, immobile and implacable, she stood, staring, as he left. An interloper.

When he reached the bridge, he relaxed. Not displeased, after all, by the outcome of his assignment. Yes, he felt a bit of guilt. But that was nothing new. He frequently felt guilt upon the completion of a successful job. Always preferable to the shame of failure.

And as for the misunderstanding with the girl, well, perhaps it was for the best that he hadn't liberated her. True, it was a disappointment. But in the end, he wasn't prepared for the sort of commitment that such a transformation implied. He'd only just turned thirty, and he had his own life to live. Better to do so without encumbrances.

He rubbed his nascent beard and began to whistle as he crossed the swamp. Forgetting the girl and the mud. The ache of his lost soul. Looking forward to his triumphant return to the village and his employers. They'd be impressed by his work. Perhaps he was finally due a promotion.

PEBBLES

PHILIPPA was an easily distracted girl. Very good at number theory. Very bad at facial recognition. Her father had given her a friendly red card to pin to her jacket should she wander off and find herself lost. Explaining to the chance stranger her unusual cognitive style. A coy request for help and understanding.

Despite the red card, Philippa's father worried about her. Small for her age, lost in her head, she was a natural target of villains whose minds weren't as finely wired as her own. Her fragility drove him to despair.

But then, so too did her isolation. Content to remain at home counting, arranging, and creating things, paltry or infinite, abstract or material, Philippa rarely ventured beyond the boundary of their cottage—a boundary marked by smooth, speckled, fist-sized stones that she adored. She played a great deal of Minecraft. Forgot, for days, to step outdoors.

Her pale face lit by a flickering screen, wan and ill after a week or two of enraptured immobility, always distressed Philippa's father. A physical man. He would devise, on these occasions, games and excuses to entice her into the air. Tasks she could undertake without causing her or, worse, himself anxiety. Small triumphs of the everyday that would counterbalance her already notable mathematical achievements. Philippa was well-known in the village for her atypical brain. Her red card.

One day, after Philippa had emerged from a particularly protracted absence in the realm of JavaScript and Leopold Kronecker, Philippa's father hit upon a project that would occupy his daughter for at least a day and a night. Return the light to her eyes. A flush to her cheeks.

His sister, who had experienced a difficult childbirth, hadn't contacted him for three days. (He worried about his sister as well.) He'd send Philippa to his sister's house in the woods with a basket of provisions. A gift. Something to restore her—his sister's—strength. Her health.

Philippa's father knew about provisions, health, and gifts of this sort because he himself produced and sold artisanal meat. Rillettes, terrines, and galantine. Pancetta, prosciutto, and guanciale. Sausage, since The Liquid Loaf went under. Chorizo and rapini. An occasional experimental merguez or black pudding. Philippa's father took his profession seriously. His meats had won awards.

And Philippa herself delighted in her father's butchery. The meats, their colors and shapes, appealed to her sense of order. But more than that, she admired his tools. The commercial slicer, polished to a brilliant sheen, five and a half feet long, capable of slicing a yellow gelbwurst half her own size into slivers thinner than a fingernail. Transparent and delicate, fanned across a brittle, blue and white ceramic serving plate. The grinder that could as easily spit out ropes of beef the diameter of a child's arm as it could the finest paste of goose liver or lamb's brain.

When her father suggested to her that she bring a basket to her aunt in the forest, she readily agreed not least because she'd be allowed—from a distance—to watch him prepare it. And once her mother had packed the meats—the patés and salumis, the bratwursts and metworsts—into the colorful straw basket, she eagerly took it under her arm. A trifle unwieldy. Unbalancing her. But full of the best her father could produce. She felt proud to be its bearer.

Her father affixed the red card to Philippa's jacket and reminded her to keep to the trail. A straight path, cleaved through the forest, that he and Philippa had explored many times before. His sister lived less than two miles away. This once, he felt little concern as he watched his daughter's frail form disappearing into the growth. She'd spend the night and return by tomorrow afternoon.

AS Philippa walked, her enthusiasm for visiting her aunt waned. Not that she didn't appreciate her father's sister: a compassionate woman who had devoted a great deal of energy to understanding her niece's condition, as she liked to call it. Having read that children like Philippa communicate more effectively via images than words, Philippa's aunt had filled her house with colorful squares of fuzzy felt to which she'd affixed Velcro ideograms—apple, cereal, sunshine; come, go, toilet, sleep—and to which she pointed, rather than speaking, when she wanted to interact with Philippa.

Filled her house, that is, aside from the workshop. Which was inviolate. Nothing close to Velcro in there. Nothing but the art.

Philippa, who found her aunt's methods of communication bewildering, had learned from experience that it was best to play along. If her aunt wanted her to point to a symbolic, fabric toilet, Philippa would humor her. If her aunt wanted her to stay away from the objects she produced in her workshop, Philippa would do so. She gazed up at the canopy that met, green and dim, over her head. But she'd rather spend the night in the forest.

She let her eyes drop to the path and identified a spike of foxglove, not yet open. Two spikes, their stems dark purple. More than a month late. Odd. A greenish pebble. She stopped and blinked. Philippa liked small rocks. Deciding that it would do no harm, she knelt at the edge of the path, set the basket carefully on the ground, and pocketed the pebble. Stood, dusted her knees, and resumed walking.

Until she spied another pebble. Red. Cuprite. She'd been reading—memorizing—a book. Unusual. She retrieved the stone and dropped it into the basket. Nestled beside the prosciutto. Her aunt wouldn't notice.

She began to return to the path, but she stopped when she noticed a small heap of pebbles a few yards into the underbrush. Gleaming in the aquamarine light of the forest. She'd never seen rocks like these in the wood. It was as though someone had been wandering, confused, scattering them.

Unable to help herself, Philippa approached the jumble of pebbles, sat cross-legged beside it, and sorted it. Twenty minutes later, she had five uneven heaps. Pink Poudretteite. White Oligoclase. Green Labradorite. Purple Iolite. A shimmery silver Hematite. Then she rubbed her eyes with her fists. She couldn't leave them here, now that she'd arranged them. But there also was no room for them in the basket.

After a guilty and surreptitious glance about the empty forest, Philippa reached beneath the layer of rillettes and removed the prosciutto. Her aunt didn't like it anyway. Then she arranged the stones by color among the remaining meats. Stood to leave. Spied another pile of stones a few feet further on.

She was sorting this larger collection of pebbles when she heard the rustling in the trees behind her. A noise situated on a perpendicular between her collection of rocks and her path. Occupied by her task, she didn't pay it attention. But when it became insistent, and closer, she turned her head.

A dog. She frowned. No, a wolf. She'd read a book about those as well. *Canis lupus.* Its head would have reached her shoulder, had she been standing, its eyes were a yellow green, its coat was dense and grey, and it was eating the prosciutto she'd left behind on the ground. When it had finished, it raised its muzzle and appraised her. She reached into the basket and found a section of chorizo. Tossed it to the wolf.

Then, pleased by the space she'd freed among the meats, she dumped the pebbles she'd collected into the bottom of the basket. Appreciated the effect. After which, resigned once more, she stood and prepared to make her way to her aunt's house.

Delighted, she spotted another, deeper, assortment of shining stones only a few yards away. Tripping over the exposed loops of an oak tree's root, she ran toward the treasure. Buried her hands in it, feeling its cool mass. Chrysoberyl and feldspar. Bronzite and Epidote. Layer upon layer of tremolite. She fell to her knees and lost herself in sorting and ordering the mineral shards. By class and by size. By color and quality. Exhilarated.

An hour later, remembering the wolf, she looked up from her work, spread now across much of the visible forest floor. The animal stood quiet and contained at the edge of her arrangement. Observing her.

With a pang of remorse at her single mindedness, her curse, Philippa stopped her categorization, found three potted pheasant terrines, and threw them to the wolf. Then, her conscience assuaged, she returned her attention to the pebbles. Counting and classifying. Until dim green gave way to black, and Philippa fell asleep.

WHEN she woke, the forest looked different. Her pebbles, she was quick to ascertain, were still in evidence, but she wasn't certain where the path lay. Straight and easy. To her aunt's house. A touch unnerved—but only a touch; her discovery of the rocks kept her brain buoyant—she rose to her feet. Noticed the wolf, still at the edge of her makeshift grid, recumbent, its chin on its paws, watching her. Distracted, she tossed it five thin links of chipolata before spinning in a full circle, fingertips out, trying to find her bearings. It didn't work.

But still, she wasn't frightened. She liked the forest. The rocks were a discovery beyond her wildest expectations. And she wouldn't, now, be forced to interact with her aunt. Her father would understand. And she knew she'd reach the end of the wood eventually. It wasn't infinite. A mathematical impossibility.

Having gathered her stones into the basket, staggering a bit under the weight, she chose a direction at random. Better than remaining still. Began trudging. The wolf, she noted without a great deal of interest, kept pace with her.

After a half hour, she dropped the basket to the ground, exhausted. It was too heavy. Irritated, she dug through its contents, found a collection of thinly sliced bresaola, ate three pieces herself, and tossed the rest to the wolf. Five minutes later, she threw it a whole kielbasa, surprised that her mother had managed to stuff so very much meat into what was, after all, a child's size basket.

And, from then on, as she walked, she dropped slices, pots, links, and chunks of meat behind her, turning back occasionally with half a smile to watch the wolf devour them. Though she never reached the end of her father's provisions, the basket became lighter, and Philippa began to enjoy herself. Imagining where she'd hide the pebbles when she'd returned home. The websites she'd visit to identify them. Some of the minerals she'd collected were incomprehensible to her. A mystery and a pleasure.

When the sun was high enough that it almost penetrated the forest canopy, Philippa stumbled across a house. Not her aunt's, she determined. Nor her father's. A wooden A-frame, abandoned, it seemed, fronted by a road and, beyond that, an overgrown open area.

Though disappointed by the absence of inhabitants—and frustrated by the uselessness of her friendly red card—Philippa nonetheless found the house enchanting. It was surrounded, submerged, by the most opulent lilies she had ever encountered. Smothered by them. Suffocating in them.

Entranced, she circled the house, followed by the wolf, and fingered the silken petals. Stood on her toes to inhale the fragrance dripping from the pollen-encrusted stamens. Rubbed a tiny, pink bell against her cheek.

The lilies would also serve a more practical purpose. Though not a devious child, Philippa recognized that she must prepare herself for a modicum of adult disappointment over her abandonment of the path. And should she find herself at her aunt's, rather than at her father's, when she did emerge from the wood, she ought to have something to present to the woman. Aside from whatever was left of the meat.

Extravagant pink and white lilies would be ideal. They also wouldn't be heavy.

Setting her basket on the A-frame's slick, moss-covered porch, Philippa set to work breaking off the stems of the more ostentatious flowers—the ones her fuzzy-felt-square-obsessed aunt might like the most. As she worked, she hummed to herself, still trailed by the wolf—to which she continued to throw the odd strip of meat—until she nearly tripped over a decaying and dreadful bit of garden art. Something sinister in the otherwise delightful, sunlit garden. The sort of thing her aunt might produce in a wicked mood.

A hunched man, she thought as she peered down at it. Though it was difficult to tell, so furred with moss and lichen was its exterior. Clearly a grotesque—a stone *gobbi*. She was familiar with *gobbi*s because her aunt carved and sold hundreds of them to tourists. Though most were larger than this. Meant to disconcert the chance garden visitor. To unsettle. She shifted her foot away from its wrathful face, inches from the ground. It did its protective job well.

She was on the verge of backing up, satisfied by what she'd gathered and flustered by the statue, when she noticed that the *gobbi* was covering, or protecting, an abundant stand of beautiful red flowers. Not lilies. Though Philippa couldn't have said what they were. She squatted for a better look. Stretched out a childish finger to prod a swollen and glistening red lip. But before she could make contact, the wolf snapped at her. Growled.

Startled, Philippa straightened. She wasn't angered by the wolf's behavior. She'd forgotten its presence, and undoubtedly it was still hungry. Time to return to her basket and find her way out of the wood in any case. Her aunt wouldn't appreciate the alien pod-like flowers. Not her style. Her aunt liked comprehensible and solid, even in her wicked moods.

Digging out three thick packets of saucisson, she nibbled at one and threw the other two to the wolf. Then she arranged the lilies in her basket, pleased by their scent as well as by the lightness of her burden, and she trudged away from the A-frame. Retracing her earlier steps. Followed by the wolf.

AS dusk fell, Philippa approached a formidable wooden structure. Porch and garden, trellis and carved wooden gate. Her aunt's house. Pushing down her disappointment—she'd hoped to find herself at her father's—she dumped the remainder of the meat on the dry dirt at the edge of the trees. To occupy the wolf. Knowing that it wasn't the sort of visitor her aunt would welcome.

Then, rearranging the lilies, she approached the front door. Where she sensed immediately that something was wrong. The trellis had been pulled down, splintered into pulpy fragments. The wooden pinecones that had decorated the gate were gone, little nubs of naked cherrywood all that remained of their smug impersonation of an actual seed. And the oak lattice surrounding the porch was wet dust. Nothing more. The hardwood slab beneath it sucked into a vortex of some sort.

Philippa cocked her head. Perhaps this was deliberate. She knew, also from experience, that her expectations of adult behavior were often flawed. And her aunt, never an easy read, may have altered the exterior of her home deliberately.

162

The design equivalent of the fuzzy felt toilet and the Velcro. The carved figures in her workshop.

Even so, Philippa climbed the stairs with more caution than she did ordinarily. And when no response answered her knock at the door, she pushed it open on quiet hinges and tiptoed inside. Holding her breath.

The inside was wrong as well. There was a smell. Metal, spittle, and wood. Something cooking that shouldn't have been. Looking down, Philippa spotted a puddle of something sticky smeared in a crude streak in the direction of the kitchen. She knelt and touched her fingertip to it. Brown and red. Congealed in places. The metallic smell deepened.

Philippa straightened and followed the streaks. Noted as she traversed the corridor that her aunt's cloth pictographs were undamaged. Three green triangles representing the forest. A yellow face with a smile. A blue face with a frown. A collection of purple grapes. The grapes were lopsided, and Philippa paused to straighten them. Then, noting that the kitchen light was on, she walked with more confidence into the large room.

But it, too, was empty. The copper pots hung silent from their hooks. The scarred butcher's block—a gift from her father—was clean and dry. Though a small corner of it had been removed, as though with a damp chisel. The brownish streaks dirtying the floor clotted into two or three deeper quagmires here on the terracotta.

Concentrated, it appeared, in the area just beneath the small oven.

Which was lit. A charred forest fire smell leaking from it. Absentminded, Philippa switched off the heat. Her aunt, like Philippa, could be forgetful. Distracted. Especially when she was occupied in her workshop. Chances were that she'd been holed up there for days, had failed to remember her cooking, and had for the same reason neglected to contact Philippa's father. Though she sympathized with her father, Philippa also understood her aunt's moods. Balked at disturbing her when she was concentrating. She hoped, vaguely, that the baby was all right.

Determined to complete her task, however, even if a day or two late, Philippa gathered her courage. Turning on her heel and leaping over the largest of the syrupy puddles, she made her way to the workshop at the back of the house. Pursed her lips at the splintered wainscoting as she passed. Surprised. Her aunt must be on something of a rampage. She rarely brought her tools beyond the boundaries of her studio. Certainly never hacked into the immaculate wood of her domestic space.

And, Philippa reminded herself as she halted on the threshold of the dark room, she never, *ever* left the door to the workshop open. Philippa ran a fingertip along the edge of the door, which had been chewed to a ragged, saw-like edge. Left hanging, gaping, on its hinges. She took a half step forward and switched on the light. Drew in her breath at the state of her aunt's creations.

The larger figures, those that had been molded from cedar trunks or fallen oak trees, were minimally damaged. Impossible to damage. But the others—the mundane, the easily purchased, the endearing childlike miniatures—had been ravaged. Some were little more than a diminutive wrist or hand, a set of eyeballs, a toe. There'd been a massacre. And in the middle of it all stood her aunt.

Philippa swallowed and approached the stationary form. Circled it to look up into her face. And understood. It was her aunt's dressing gown, but not her aunt. Though Philippa was bad at faces, even she could see that this thing couldn't be her father's sister. The ears hung too long, the eyes bulged too wide, the hands too large and the mouth far, far too broad. Not her aunt. One of her aunt's creations.

A specialist in ears and eyes, hands and lips, Philippa's aunt made them big. Some of the less ponderous sculptures—those most beloved by the tourists—were *only* ears, teeth, and hands. A planter sporting a twisted, knobby thumb or thumbnail. An earlobe. A candleholder sprouting up from a thick fang and lip. Philippa's aunt had an eye for that sort of beauty.

Whatever her creative instincts, however, she was not home now. Philippa knew that she'd never have allowed her workshop to fall into its current disarray had she been present. And as for the dressing gown on the carving, it was another adult mystery that Philippa chose not to ponder.

Rather, gathering up her basket and switching off the light, she left the workshop and the house. Found her path. A straight, easy journey back to her father's. Out of the bewildering forest.

WHEN Philippa reached the border of speckled stones—touching each as she passed—and then the door to her own cottage, her father and mother rushed out to greet her. As her mother took the basket from her, her father unpinned the red card from her jacket. Kissed her head.

"You're half a day late, Philippa," he said. "Did you know that?"

"Yes," she admitted.

"My sister forgot to telephone?"

Philippa blinked. Yes. This was easier than trying to explain the iolite and beryl. The feldspar and topaz. The wolf. The dressing gown. "Yes."

"Typical." He draped his arm across her shoulder and followed her mother inside.

Her mother, removing the lilies from the basket, smiled at the accumulation of pebbles beneath them. Handed the basket to Philippa. "These belong to you, I presume?"

Philippa nodded. Retrieved the basket.

Her mother arranged the lilies in a vase. "And these are from your aunt? They're lovely."

"No," said Philippa. "She wasn't there. In the house, I mean. I gathered the flowers in the forest."

Her father frowned. "I thought you said she'd forgotten to telephone."

166

"Oh." Philippa looked at her shoes. "No. That wasn't true. I'm sorry."

"Then where did the meat go?" Her father was more curious than angry.

"The wolf ate it." Philippa ran her fingertips over the top layer of her pebbles.

"Philippa—" began her mother. But then her eyes widened. She knelt and examined the girl's shoes. "Good Heavens. Is that blood?"

Her father also peered down at his daughter's shoes. Philippa, obliging, dropped her basket, removed a shoe, and handed it to her mother.

"It *is* blood."

"Philippa," said her father, "where did this happen?"

"Aunt's house."

He and her mother exchanged a look. "She said there'd been a wolf. I've heard rumors of one prowling recently. I didn't believe them."

"But it wouldn't attack a woman in her own home."

"You know my sister—"

"Oh God, the baby—"

"Philippa," said her father, "would you play in your room while your mother and I talk?"

Good. She wanted to re-examine her pebbles. Nodding, she left her parents to their conversation.

THE next morning, Philippa woke early enough to overhear her parents murmuring in their bedroom. Through the cottage wall. She curled up in her bed, smiling, as their words drifted across her watery consciousness. This was her favorite time of the day. Treasured because she so often missed it.

"...not much left of her," her father was saying. "It had cached her in the oven, if you can believe it. And then somehow the oven had been lit as well. But she was identifiable."

"I'm so sorry." The sound of her mother hugging her father.

"She was bound to end badly. She was my sister, and I feel a certain loyalty. But she wasn't right in the head." He paused. "Those carvings—"

"What about the baby?"

He laughed. Bitter. "Nothing could harm that baby. You know that."

"And?"

"God knows."

"At least you tracked the wolf. I'm proud of you, darling."

"It was a joint effort." He cleared his throat. "Larger than any of us thought. Thank God Philippa was unhurt." He paused again. "They let me keep the carcass. For the skin. Do you think she'd like it in her room? As a rug or a blanket or something like that? It wouldn't frighten her, would it?"

Philippa hugged herself in the bed. Though she hadn't paid it much attention, she'd grown attached to the wolf. Enjoyed its company. Having it in her room with her, always, would be delightful. She squeezed her eyes shut, slipping back into an early morning sleep. Her father understood everything.

THORNS

GRUSS an Aachen. Fluffy and fully double. Peach and creamy white. He clipped three stems. Inhaled the scent. Moved on. Cécile Brünner. Small and pink. Fading to wallpaper yellow. He clipped five. Lady Hillingdon. Orange and exuberant. He tilted back his head and shaded his eyes with a hand. Waxy buds. Heady fragrance. He flourished his secateurs and then paused. Uncertain. Replaced the blades in a back pocket. He'd leave Lady Hillingdon alone for today. What he'd cut was sufficient.

Patting a stem, familiar and proprietary, he pricked his thumb, winced, and sucked at the wound. Retreated, quiet and stealthy, from the room, leery of disturbing its occupants. Remarkable that such ebullient roses could grow indoors. Confined as they were to a single, stifling, if well-lit, tower. Bower.

Not that his home leant itself to distinctions between outward and inward. Exterior and interior. Path and dead-end. He closed and locked the door. Walked along the muffled carpet, appreciating as he always did its infinitely variable lynx motif. Listened to his hedge. His visitor was nearer this morning. Still a day or two off. But closer. He could feel it through the briars.

He descended to the floor below and checked on his investments. Bigger. He really ought to find them a larger room. Tugging the door closed with two hands, he walked further on. Glanced out a mullioned window. Frowned. The view had changed again. What had been a wall of jagged, hooked solanum—purple thorns and tangerine berries, deadly to the touch and taste— had been replaced by an elephantine hops plant. Iridescent green flowers like paper lanterns hanging over some unhallowed circus.

A marauding tendril had cracked one of the panes of the window. He reached up to push it back outside, and it encircled his wrist, iron-hard, cutting off the circulation to his hand. Thinking quickly, he grabbed his secateurs with his free hand and cut through the stem. Pulled back his arm and unwrapped the limp green thread from his wrist. Pleased. He was anything but averse to the aggression of bines.

As he turned, he noticed that the plant had regrouped and sent three runners coiling to the floor, slithering in the direction of the east wing. The wrong direction. They'd be stymied when they reached the black, windowless corridor that joined the two parts of the house. But he admired their resolution nonetheless.

He descended further, to the ground floor, greeted his cat—briefly; it was on its way elsewhere—and wandered into his drawing room. Poured himself a glass of whisky, though it was early, and gazed out the tall windows at the maze. Frowned again.

It too had changed. The entrance—exit, point-of-view was not his strength—was now on the far left. And inside, he could make out a towering pyramid of multiflora roses that hadn't been there the night before. Invasive.

He sighed. Hoped the altered topography wouldn't delay his visitor too dramatically. The man's—he assumed it was a man—hostility was palpable from well over a mile away, and the despair was beginning to grate. Undoubtedly also provoking the ire of the hedge. A jumpy bit of greenery even under the best of circumstances. Talius wondered what was so important that the man felt the need to hack his way through a proverbially impenetrable briar to reach him. But he'd be enlightened soon enough.

Then, remembering himself, he set his whisky on a piano bench, crossed to a vase of wilted roses that sat on the mantelpiece of a pink marble fireplace, and removed the old stems. Tossed the stems into the hearth, filled the vase

with clean water from a pitcher, and arranged the
fresh flowers. Sniffed Cécile Brünner. Downed the
remainder of his whisky and forced himself into
action. He was in need of flax. To greet his visitor.
Whenever his visitor might finally make an
appearance.

TALIUS grew his flax in a rocky plot of
thin, unhealthy soil on the south side of the house.
He disliked the area. Insignificant, weedy little
plant. Unremarkable blue flowers. He'd much
prefer to replace the meagre, whitish dirt with
something dark and nutritious—blood and bone.
The weeds with something delicate and
demanding. But the flax was crucial to his
enterprise. Without it, everything about him would
crumble.

And at least the plot didn't move. Unlike
his roses, his hedge, his labyrinth, his carpets, the
windows of his house even, the flax stayed put.
Though he pulled at it with a certain contempt,
therefore, it was a relief to rest in its midst for an
hour or two after having passed the remainder of
his time treading on carpets that refused to repeat,
observing vistas that refused to reflect the proper
time of day, and tending to roses that changed size,
color, and petal-count between dawn and noon.
This bit of ground was too degraded to flirt with
him. It was an area he could dominate.

He refused to dress for the flax. Wore
neither hat nor gloves. Rather, having pulled on
tweed trousers and a pink poplin shirt, he marched

out to the plot, detached what he needed, shoved it into a brown paper bag, and returned to the kitchen to prepare it. He paused and inhaled the brambles as he passed. Exhaled, irritated. The man was still a day away. He must be a particularly dimwitted example of his type. As they increasingly were.

THE next morning, Talius squeezed himself a glass of orange juice while looking out on a shed-sized, pink bougainvillea that hadn't been in his drive the night before. It had sprouted in the center of the circular brick apron that no one, ever, used. An unpleasant, medicinal pink. He thought he might go after it with an axe once he'd breakfasted. Something to occupy him until his visitor arrived. He was estimating, now, late afternoon. Perhaps the man would enjoy taking tea with him.

Talius dawdled throughout the remainder of the morning watering and fertilizing the roses that grew in the south-facing rooms of the third floor and clipping back those that climbed the exterior of the northwest tower of the east wing. Slapping back the occasional probing tendril or cane. Collecting an armful of white Pascali blooms that had recently opened.

Then, rolling up the sleeves of an old, flannel work-shirt, he donned a straw hat to keep off the sun and dug his axe out of the potting shed. Double-headed. Bronze. Not the most efficient tool for an upstart bougainvillea, but Talius was

174

used to the old thing. He balanced it fondly in his palm before obliterating the fuchsia monstrosity that had blighted his otherwise spare and calming drive.

As he was dragging the bleeding sprigs and boughs, losing the occasional traumatized leaf, in the direction of his compost heap, he stopped, frustrated. Dropped his burden to the ground and squinted upward. The briar had changed again. The exit—entrance, whatever—was now a small, arched passageway situated directly at the center, and the teetering column of multiflora roses had been pushed to the extreme edge, threatening what he knew was a public road.

He removed his hat and fanned his face with it. Though obviously he never perspired. "Would you please," he said, "simply let the man through? I no longer find this amusing. And I will retaliate if I become irritated."

A shiver of what might have been a breeze passed along the top of the hedge. Back again. Talius replaced his hat, gathered up the repellent bougainvillea, and disposed of it. Then, pleased by his day's accomplishments he returned to the house to change his clothing. Prepare for his visitor. Set out a few tempting teacakes. On his way, he tossed his axe back into a corner of the shed.

At three in the afternoon, there was a knock at his front door. Peremptory. Belligerent. Talius sighed again. The man was hopeless. He ran a hand through his hair, shooed his cat into another room, crossed his echoing hall, and opened the door.

Stifled yet another sigh. Though he'd been expecting his guest to show signs of wear after his adventure through the briars, he was unprepared for the abject state of the man on his doorstep. The man's eyes were not only angry and accusatory, but just this side of deranged. His hair stood on end and was littered with shards of glass and the egg sac of what Talius believed was a huntsman spider. His clothing was tattered, hanging off of him by threads. A surreptitious examination, however, convinced Talius that it hadn't been particularly impressive before its encounter with his roses. Cheap dye. Some sort of blend.

Talius stood to the side. "Won't you come in? May I take your spiders?"

"What?"

"Your—um." Talius flushed. He hated socializing with idiots. Then, with a delicate twist of his fingertips, he disengaged the spider sac from the man's tangled hair. Held it out. "Would you like to keep it?"

The man stared.

"I'll leave it here with the umbrellas, then." Talius set the white, gently vibrating sphere on the edge of the umbrella stand. "Come in?" Hopeful.

Sullen, the man stepped over the threshold. Talius let out the breath he hadn't realized he'd been holding and moved to shut the door. As he passed the man, however, he froze. Astonished.

ON THE NATURE OF THINGS

The man was missing his soul. A great gaping void. Certainly not the work of his hedge, which was a superficial piece of shrubbery even at its most menacing. Something more malevolent had done this to him. Something with a grudge.

He pushed the door closed, turned, and looked sidelong at the man, who was examining the hall with aggressive indifference. Attempting, badly, to appear unimpressed. Talius colored more deeply. The man seemed to be unaware of his soul's absence. Blithe. If anything, he was more confident in his skin than Talius himself was.

Talius gestured toward the drawing room, where he'd set out the tea. He wasn't going to mention it if the man himself didn't. Besides, the man also was wearing a four-day growth of beard that Talius suspected wasn't the product of his recent exertions in the labyrinth. A more serious lack of decorum than the missing soul, in Talius's view, and suggestive of a certain—insensitivity—to his personal presentation. His outward aspect. "Tea?"

The man glowered at him. Didn't move. "No. Thanks. I've come here in an official capacity."

"Oh?" Talius dropped his arm. "I'm Talius."

"Ash."

"How do you do?"

"Right." The man held Talius's eyes. "I'm a private investigator. A fixer."

"Oh?" Talius cocked his head. The man, from what he sensed, could read or speak one hundred twelve languages. Give or take. A strange job for a person with his skill set. "You've come to investigate, then? To—fix—something?"

"A number of women have gone missing from the forest." Ash watched Talius for a reaction. "We've received information that you might know what's become of them."

"Oh." Relieved. "Yes, of course. Would you like to see them now? Or after tea—?"

Ash blinked. Not, it seemed, expecting this reply. "Now is good."

"Very well." Talius led Ash toward the wide, carpeted staircase, grabbing and pocketing his secateurs along the way. Noticed Ash gaping at his cat, which had slunk back from wherever it had hidden itself. Pushed the cat into the music room, embarrassed, and continued up the stairs. "Shall we begin on the first floor and work upward?"

"Yes, fine."

Talius glanced behind him as Ash reached the landing. "Mind the bine."

"What?" And then: "shit."

"Oh dear." Talius cut through the stem that had wrapped itself around Ash's ankle. Moving upward. Inappropriate. The plant had rumbled the east wing, apparently. He replaced the secateurs. "Sorry. It showed up yesterday. I've no idea what it wants."

"Yesterday?" Ash was straightening the tattered cuff of his badly cut trousers.

ON THE NATURE OF THINGS

"Hmm. Utterly devastated the solanum, unfortunate thing." Talius had stopped before a locked door. Retrieving a set of keys from his other pocket, he opened it, half turning to address Ash. But then, before he could speak, he jumped and shut the door again. From behind it came the deafening shriek of caged birds. A small mink slithered out between his legs. "Whoops. Wrong door. So sorry."

Embarrassed again, he continued along the hall until he reached a corner room at the end. Took a breath and pushed open the door. A rope of flesh the size and consistency of a child's inflatable pool toy burst from the gap and unspooled over the carpet. Amorphous and unthinkable. But also living. Breathing. Stinking of banana-flavored Suzy Q's. Talius looked a question at Ash. Wondering whether this was what he wanted to see.

But Ash, his hand over his mouth, merely stumbled backward. Shook his head. Closed his eyes and emitted an odd squeaking sound.

Disappointed, Talius gathered the flesh into both arms, crammed it back into the room, and pulled the door closed again. "Right. Well, that one's difficult to parse. Let's try upstairs, shall we?"

Ash nodded, dumb, and followed his host. Talius led him to the next floor without mishap and opened the proper door on the first try. Gestured inside. Hopeful once again.

Here, there was both space and air. But hanging in the air was the overpowering scent of funerals and inheritances; and the space was overrun by the flaking branches of an unusual flat purple rose. Prominent at the center of it all was an exquisite glass coffin, the inside of which was a solid mass of green.

"I'll remove the lid?" Talius indicated the latch.

Ash nodded once more. But when he understood what lived beneath the glass, he flinched a second time and hid his face in his hands. It was a girl. Flawless skin. Black hair. Tiny feet. Sweet breath. And from her open mouth, her wrists, her belly, and the underside of her thighs, grew delicate, insistent sprouts of roses. Miniature thorns. Infant buds and leaves.

Talius replaced the coffin's lid. "The glass keeps them warm," he said. "Until they're old enough to transplant outside. Fend for themselves." And then, misunderstanding Ash's silence: "no need to worry, the stag is out there too. It's fine. Well occupied by the briar, I believe."

Ash dropped his fingers from his face. "What?"

"The stag." Confused by the lack of comprehension. "Her brother." Talius waited. When Ash failed to reply, he half shrugged. Bored by the stupidity. "Shall we continue?"

They reached the third floor, and Talius showed Ash into a dark, ponderous room like a second-class suite in a formerly fashionable hotel. Heavy gold curtains. Red and blue carpet. Solid, four-poster bed. On which slept a woman who had briefly made the local news.

"The mother," Ash murmured. "Of the two kids. The kids with the problems. I know this one."

"Yes, you *do* know this one." As though addressing a slow and benighted toddler. Talius had begun to worry that his guest was not only mad—to be expected after his time in the hedge— but pathologically simpleminded.

"I purchased her from the husband," Talius explained. "Ordinarily, I wouldn't have bothered, but she came cheap. And I'm confident that once she's regained a bit of weight, she'll do for the Dicentra. They're perfectly happy without nutrients, and I can keep her in the shade. Which she appears to prefer."

He indicated a frail tuft of fernlike growth under the woman's chin. "You see? This one has already taken. Sweet little thing."

He smiled at Ash, inviting him to appreciate the sprightly, green tissue. When Ash simply stared, he nodded, resigned once more, and beckoned. "This way."

Ash shook his head and came out of whatever trance had paralyzed him. "She was ill," he said to Talius. "She'd slipped into a coma. She was vegetative."

"They're all *vegetative.*" Irritated. "*This* way."

Ash followed Talius without demur. Tripped on the carpet as he climbed to the floor above. Paused to peer at a frozen, bluish girl wearing a winter hat and standing on a platform. Stuffed into an alcove.

"No, no," Talius remarked, pointing further along the corridor. "That's just art." He turned away. "I picked it up from that agoraphobic brewer. Thought it had a certain atmosphere about it."

They stopped before the rounded wall of another tower room. "You'll enjoy this one."

He opened the door. Asphyxiating scent of a thousand different roses, all open, all unusually large, all facing—oddly—away from the windows. Watching them. A malign room. And at the center of it, on a wide silk bed was a woman, herself half-smothered by a sprawling apricot Alchymist and also half-smothered by an enormous cat with tufted ears and blinding, multicolored footpads. Entirely smothered, in other words.

Talius gestured toward the scene and began to speak, but Ash interrupted him. "No. Stop it. Don't say anything. I don't want to know."

Talius closed his mouth. And then, meek: "but there are so many more. It's a large house. Lots of roses. Wouldn't you rather—"

"I've seen enough."

Talius nodded, followed him out of the room, and eased the door shut. "Tea, then?"

"Yes. Thank you. I'd like that."

ON THE NATURE OF THINGS

WHEN they were both seated at the round, baroque table, walnut inlaid with rose, Talius risked resuming the conversation. He was drinking Darjeeling tea. His guest had preferred a glass of whisky. It seemed not to be doing him much good.

"Are you satisfied with your investigation, then? Nothing more I can show you?" Talius took a delicate bite of rosewater manchet. "Anything more to, er, fix?"

"Why do you do it?" Ash deposited his empty tumbler on the table with clumsy force. "What could possibly motivate you to do—that—to people?"

"Ah." Talius smiled. "Well, that's an easy one."

"Oh?"

"Indeed." He leaned back in the chair and settled his ankle on his knee. "It's a family curse."

When Ash merely stared, he continued. "They say that some ancestor of mine offended a malevolent fairy." His smile turned to a grin. "Imagine that." Then he wrinkled his forehead. "Something about insufficient cutlery."

Ash gazed down at the four forks, two knives, and five small spoons, all heavy gold, that surrounded his china tea plate. He'd used none of them. "Insufficient cutlery."

"Something like that." Talius considered. "Ever since then, anyone who comes near us sinks into a profound lethargy. Ten miles in every direction." He paused. "Not to mention our ongoing difficulties with the hedge."

"Those women aren't asleep." Resolute. Aggressive.

Talius pushed down another smile. "It will happen to you too, you know."

"You've been using them, instrumentalizing them—"

"'Instrumentalizing.' I like that word." And then: "at least we're not cannibals."

" *What?*"

"We don't cook and eat—" he shook his head. "Never mind."

Ash began to reply, but before the sound emerged, his face relaxed. Went simple, slack, and serene. A look that Talius knew well.

A few seconds later, gathering his energy, Ash raised his hand half an inch from the tabletop. Stared across at Talius. And crashed forward onto his plate. His forehead shattering it.

Talius tensed. "Oh dear. There's another place setting gone." He contemplated the top of Ash's head. The shards of glass. A lone spider, which he coaxed onto his fingertip and then allowed to spin itself to the ground. "It's in the flax, you see. Something about the flax—inside of you—"

Ash didn't respond. But then, Talius didn't expect him to. Rather, he mulled over how he would spend the evening. Moving his visitor upstairs would be troublesome. And he'd never worked with a man before. Though his

184

grandmother had had luck with that small one from the Catskills in her day.

And on the other side of the equation, Talius knew precisely the rose to introduce once Ash was in place. "Honor." A tall, white hybrid tea. Disease resistant.

He stood and rolled back his shoulders. Popped the final piece of manchet into his mouth. Before he did anything, he'd shave off the disfiguring stubble. Aesthetically catastrophic effect.

As he wandered upstairs in search of a razor, he patted the cat's head. Pity he couldn't do anything about the missing soul. Though obviously the roses wouldn't notice. "Honor" couldn't care less whether the man was empty inside. It was the blood and the bone that mattered. And Ash had more than enough of that to spare. Enough for anyone.

QUILLS

DOROTHEA dropped her chainsaw to the ground, lifted her safety goggles, and wiped a tear from her cheek. Tried to expunge the image of the nursing infant from her mind. Its closed eyes. Its soft tuft of hair. The clutching, vulnerable fingers. She'd seen it again—an advertisement for fabric softener or dryer sheets, a product she couldn't remember and would never use—that morning as she'd skimmed her anachronistic newspaper. Had vowed to pay it no attention. Had broken down sobbing. Hormones.

Now, her work on the house-sized goblin, a carving she was hacking out of three felled Douglas Firs, was wrecked for the day. Again. She couldn't concentrate on her art, on the things she coaxed and pulled and compelled from the wood, with the ghostly baby taunting her.

186

ON THE NATURE OF THINGS

She'd always told herself that birthing the trolls and the giants, the *gobbi* and the brownies, the odd undine, was fertility enough for her. No different from whatever her body might cobble together, except that she maintained creative control. For the past seven or eight months, however, her brain chemicals had been launching a counter attack. At the moment, they appeared to be winning.

Not that Dorothea had put up a particularly vigorous fight. On more than one occasion—on fifty-three occasions, to be exact—she'd allowed the male tourists who purchased her wares—usually her sylphs and nymphs rather than her gnomes and salamanders, male tourists being what they are—into the back room of her workshop. To sample her additional wares. Spread out on a bed of sawdust and woodchips. The fragrance of wounded cedar boughs flavoring the air. They called her a witch.

Witch or not, however, the accident for which she'd been preparing herself—though the thought of it was never allowed to push its way into her cerebral cortex, to rub supraliminal shoulders with her artistic impulses—failed to materialize. At one point, she'd even purchased a stick that changed its color. But it hadn't changed. Inert and uniformly beige. Nothing more than a stick.

Now, driving the steel toe of her work boot into the incompletely fashioned lower leg of the faceless goblin, she strode to the picnic table on which she kept her bottled water and waste paper.

Necessary for calming her circular saws when they became jumpy. Flipped through the old edition of the journal published by that obscure geographical society—an outstanding source of scrap—to find the other advertisement that she'd marked.

Accidentally marked. Uncertain as to how, why, or even when she'd encountered the tiny notice. An advertisement for a fertility clinic. On the other side of the forest, beyond her brother's cottage.

WHAT you must understand, Miss—"

"Dorothea." Dorothea, still wearing her steel-toed boots, her canvas coveralls, and the safety glasses on her forehead, sat in the antiseptic consulting room of the clinic. Hating the chilly woman who was haranguing her. The fertility doctor. A woman as far from reproductive as any Dorothea could imagine. Inorganic. Not biological. But Dorothea didn't want to antagonize her. The woman had something that Dorothea desired. A child. "Dorothea is fine."

"Yes," said the woman, resettling her glasses on her nose. "Dorothea. What you must understand is that the procedure is experimental. Highly experimental. We've yet to find a patient willing to undergo the risks—"

"I'm willing to undergo the risks."

"Ah." The woman cleared her throat. "There is a good chance that the child will be—different."

"I like different." Dorothea stared across at the woman. "I'm different."

"And you would be asked to undergo extensive hormone therapy before we even began work on the embryonic cells—"

"Fine," repeated Dorothea. "Tell me how it works."

"Excellent." The woman's face moved in what Dorothea assumed was meant to be a smile. "The procedure makes use of the ongoing research into the hedgehog signaling pathway. Are you familiar with this term?"

"Yes," said Dorothea, who had come prepared. "The first hedgehog gene was isolated in fruit flies, drosophila—"

"No. Not fruit flies. *Hedgehogs.*"

"It's called the 'hedgehog' signaling pathway because—"

"—because the tissues and hormones are derived from hedgehogs," finished the woman. "Quite correct."

Dorothea, who wasn't an expert, closed her mouth. Gestured for the woman to continue.

"We recommend a course of hedgehog hormone therapy for three of your cycles before we introduce the embryonic cells." She consulted a desk calendar. "If we begin this afternoon, we might conceivably schedule the initial fertilization for the twenty-first of April." She glanced up. "Acceptable?"

"Yes." Dorothea was having difficulty damping down her excitement. An infant.

Something from her own body. To nurse. To shape.

"I ought to make you cognizant of the potential side-effects," continued the woman.

"All right."

"As I mentioned earlier, the child may develop unusually. I won't say 'abnormally,' because we expect certain differences in a fetus formed half or more from hedgehog genetic material." She motioned Dorothea into silence. "Additionally, however, you yourself might undergo a few changes. It's difficult to know which will present. But you may—" she lifted her glasses to read from a pamphlet on the desk in front of her, "crave small animal proteins, shift to nocturnal habits, and produce excess saliva."

She paused. "Oh, and it's likely that you'll develop a mild immunity to snake and spider venom. But best not test that." The facial twitch that could have been a smile. "You see? It's not all bad."

Dorothea clasped her hands together in her lap. "I understand."

"You consent to undergo the treatment, then?" The woman gazed across the desk at Dorothea.

"Yes."

She opened a desk drawer, retrieved a document, and pushed it toward Dorothea. "Sign here, and we'll commence immediately."

ON THE NATURE OF THINGS

FOUR months later, having undergone her hormone treatment and successfully bonded with the embryo, Dorothea went into labor on the tenth of June. She'd had no interest in perpetuating her relationship with the wintry staff of the fertility clinic, and so she had severed contact with them early on, once it was established that she was with child. Threatening a lawsuit when their furtive excitement over the speed with which the fetus was developing mushroomed into vague claims that her uterus was their intellectual property.

She knew that her gestation period would be short—the hedgehog influence. But she cared not a whit for the teratological reasons behind it or for the excitement of the clinicians and researchers who were watching it. The thing inside of her was her child. And when the time drew near, she contacted a colleague with a pottery wheel who dabbled in midwifery. A woman similarly uninterested in the patriarchal underpinnings of medical and scientific rationalism.

Unfortunately, the midwife remained with Dorothea only through two thirds of the birthing process. Already in incomprehensible pain, bleeding profusely from her vagina, feeling not only that her insides were cracking apart, which she understood was normal, but also that a thousand razor blades were grating them, she'd looked up into the potter's—midwife's—terrified eyes as the baby's head had emerged. And the midwife—potter—had made a strangled, ribbiting sound, burst into tears, and fled the room.

Dorothea had heard the front door slamming even as she herself screamed in agony and terror at the bleeding shreds of her cervix being dragged into the air along with the baby, which was now pushing and scrabbling its way to freedom. Two more contractions, and the baby was out, followed by a flux of clotted blood, ribbons of blue and purple flesh, and a large part of Dorothea's uterine wall.

Though she was faint from lack of blood and in shock from the pain, Dorothea bent forward to scoop up her child. But then, her hands lacerated, she dropped it to the floor. It was covered in needle-sharp quills. Its legs and lower body shaped essentially as a human's—a boy, she noted in passing—and its head and arms a hedgehog's. All, however, coated with deadly spines.

Weeping, hating herself for having instinctively pushed away her boy upon his first entry into the world, she felt about on her bedside table for the canvas work gloves she never left far behind, pulled them onto her hands, and—gently, tenderly—lifted the baby to her breast. His quills punctured and stabbed the skin of her chest and belly, but she sucked in her breath and endured. Cried—with joy, now—as he found what he was seeking and began to drink. She was nursing her child. Her boy. Joe, her hedgehog.

JOE grew and matured quickly once he was in the world, as a hedgehog should. A few weeks after he was born, he lost his baby quills in preparation for a thicker, more menacing coat. At four weeks, he was walking on legs that, aside from the spines, looked like an eighteen-month-old human's. And at six weeks, he was talking. More, Dorothea was smug to note, than could be said for her niece with the developmental problems. His speech was measured, quiet, and educated. A pleasure to hear.

He had, additionally, both artistic and musical talent. After begging his mother for bagpipes—an odd request—she'd presented him with his desire on the tenth of August, his two-month birthday. Delighted, he'd spent the remainder of the day hidden at the top of a tree, playing mournful airs and eating slugs, while his mother returned, inspired now, to her workshop.

In the evenings, he'd huddle in her lap, curled up on the Kevlar and spider silk apron she'd purchased for that purpose, while she read to him stories of famous hedgehogs. The hedgehog and the fox. The hedgehog and the hare. Several variations on "the hedgehog bride" that she wasn't certain were appropriate, but that she recited to him, with excisions, nonetheless. They were very happy.

Even in the midst of their happiness, however, Joe, to his shame, nourished a secret. In addition to having matured intellectually and physically a bit more quickly than was commonplace, he'd also matured emotionally. Psychologically.

He wanted companionship. Companionship of the sort that his mother skipped over in the stories, but that he knew existed, not only from the vague urges that tormented him, but from the fact that he could read complex, adult writing in four different languages. Still, he felt it best to humor her. To remain a child for at least a few weeks longer. He was sorry for his mother.

And so, in the afternoons and evenings that his mother spent in her workshop, Joe ventured secretly into the forest. Seeking he wasn't certain what. Searching and questing. Playing his bagpipes.

On these journeys, among or beyond the trees, he encountered innumerable outlandish creatures and figures, none of which, however, was what he needed. For example:

Wolves and lilies.

A silent old woman who spun him a molecule-thin coat of spider silk, specially tailored for each of his twitching quills.

An overgrown meadow of calendula and clover, viola and arugula, under which, so they said, a hellish brewer bided his time in a stinking underworld.

An A-frame house, invisible beneath its carpet of moss and lichen, beside which a petrified gnome tended his glistening red orchids.

A wall of thorns and roses that towered above the tallest cedar, and against which an angry man missing his soul battled, eternally.

ON THE NATURE OF THINGS

A dishonest lynx, a trickster, with garishly colored feet.

A bridge beneath which a troll forged words that no one would ever hear.

A roiling green vine—bine—from which Joe slowly retreated, backward, mistaking it for the serpent that encircles the world. Hedgehogs and serpents don't get on.

A little girl—

One day, when Joe was sitting at the top of a tree, playing his bagpipes, contemplating his evening journey, the tree on which he sat shuddered. He stopped playing and looked about himself, confused. After two or three minutes, convinced that he'd imagined the tremor, he took up his pipes once more.

The tree shook again. And then came a sawing sound, quite unlike the exuberant hacking and buzzing that emerged from his mother's studio. He looked down. Far beneath him, kneeling on the forest floor, was a pink and blonde girl, eating the tree.

Bemused, Joe lowered himself from the branch. The girl scrambled to her feet, backed up, and appraised him. Without fear. Without surprise. As though a half-boy, half-hedgehog, with the wrong end on top, were entirely normal to her. She smelled of moss and meadow grass, birch bark and the pollen of maple trees. His quills quivered.

"Hello," he said. "I'm Joe."

The girl blinked at him. "I'm hungry."

He liked her voice. The sound that his mother tried—and, though he'd never tell her, failed—to recreate in her carvings. The sound of callous wood. "I can see that." He moved to the side. "I don't need the tree. Eat it if you'd like."

"I'd eat it anyway," she said.

"Oh."

She ate the tree. It took her forty-five minutes. Then, sated for the moment, she turned back to him. "I'm worried about my brother. He's hungry too."

"Can I help?"

"Maybe."

She led him into the forest. Where he saw the boy—an older, more dignified, and weaker copy of the girl—leaning against a tree. Joe sensed that the boy wouldn't survive much longer in his current state. Something must be done. He looked at the girl.

"What does he need?"

"Wood." She rubbed her eyes. A childish movement that Joe found endearing, though he knew she'd resent his reaction.

"There's wood everywhere."

"No." She shook her head. "Worked wood. Carved wood. Varnished and painted wood. Old wood." She cogitated. "*Artistic* wood."

"I see." Joe made a decision. "I think I can help."

THREE evenings later, Dorothea was nursing Joe upstairs in her bedroom. Though the boy didn't need it—there were more than enough slugs for him in the forest—she continued to feed him, despite the pain, despite the blood all over her bedding, because she felt it brought them closer together. After all, the child was less than four months old. An infant. He needed his mother's milk.

She leant back on the pillows, her eyes closed, a pained crease on her brow—when she heard the sound. Again. The sawing, chiseling sound—not a wolf, but something similar—outside their door. She sat up. Moved Joe to the side, lacerating an unprotected inner wrist.

"I'm going to see what it is."

"Don't, mother," he said. "I'm certain it's only the wind."

"Nonsense." She stood and adjusted her dressing gown. "You've said that every night it's happened. And every morning, another bit of our front porch has gone. I won't put up with it any longer."

Joe rolled into a ball, his comfort position. "All right, mother."

He knew what was coming. And he felt sad about it. But also resigned. It was time.

He listened for the confrontation. Soon enough, it came. First, the sound of his mother marching down the wooden stairs. Creaking through the corridor. Opening the front door. And then: "you poor children. Are you hungry? There's more to eat inside."

The door closing. Footsteps. Moving toward the kitchen. "This way, children."

A few seconds after that, a commotion. Something hitting the wooden floor. Hard. The sound of kitchen tools. Cutting tools. A murmured conversation.

Joe realized that he wasn't merely sad; he was very sad. Sadder than he'd ever been before. Surprised by his reaction, he began to keen. A hedgehog sound. Louder and louder, though he'd always known this end was inevitable.

Two or three minutes later, he collected himself and quieted to a wet snuffling—also a hedgehog sound. It was then that he heard the footsteps. Confident. On the stairway. Climbing higher and higher.

A moment later, the door to the bedroom opened. The boy, bland and recovered, though drenched with blood, gazed at Joe. "It's finished."

"Yes," said Joe, uncurling, standing, and straightening his spider-silk coat. "I heard."

The boy glanced about the room. "It's a nice house."

"Thank you. I like it."

"But still, you want to come with us?"

"Yes," said Joe. He thought for a moment. "I want to seek my fortune."

The End

Also From Tiny Boar Books

The Thirteen Trials of Dr. Marion Bailey
by Felicity St. John

Scholar, spy, and Gothic heroine…Marion Bailey reads like Iris Murdoch or Muriel Spark re-inventing Indiana Jones and George Smiley.

Dr. Marion Bailey has had a checkered career, from the moment she washed up in 1927, a failed scholar blindsided by the brutality of the British Mandate in Iraq to her final adventure in 1938, persecuted by a demonic gibbon conjured up out of a medieval Arabic bestiary. But throughout her tribulations, she's dragged along with her the same traits and wounds: a tortured genius for decoding obscure dead languages, a fragile psyche increasingly battered by each of her exploits, and a tormented responsiveness to the medieval detritus churned up in her wake—and then gobbled up by the British Museum.

Now, in 1967, her forty-year-old son has discovered among this detritus—the five-hundred-year-old Ottoman Book of Kings, the eleventh-century Fatimid pearl of enormous size, the thirteenth-century Ilkhanid celestial globe, and the amorous golem cobbled together by an illegitimate French Queen and a Nabatean magician of ill repute—a manuscript that even his mother refused to touch. As he decides whether to take up the silent challenge posed by the sealed book, he slips backward in time, appraising, finally, his mother's troubled history.